ESCAPE TO MASADA

Escape to
Masada

LEFT BEHIND
>THE KIDS<

Jerry B. Jenkins

Tim LaHaye

WITH CHRIS FABRY

TYNDALE HOUSE PUBLISHERS, INC.
WHEATON, ILLINOIS

Visit Tyndale's exciting Web site at www.tyndale.com

Discover the latest Left Behind news at www.leftbehind.com

Published in association with the literary agency of Alive Communications, Inc., 7680 Goddard Street, Suite 200, Colorado Springs, CO 80920.

Edited by Lorie Popp

ISBN 0-8423-5801-3, mass paper

Printed in the United States of America

08 07 06 05 04 03
8   7   6   5   4   3   2   1

To Steve, Kelli, Chloe, and Mallory

TABLE OF CONTENTS

THE YOUNG TRIBULATION FORCE

Original members—Vicki Byrne, Judd Thompson, Lionel Washington

Other members—Mark, Conrad, Darrion, Janie, Charlie, Shelly, Melinda

OTHER BELIEVERS

Jim Dekker—GC satellite operator helping the kids

Chang Wong—Chinese teenager working in New Babylon

Cheryl Tifanne—pregnant young lady from Iowa

Westin Jakes—pilot for singer Z-Van

Tsion Ben-Judah—Jewish scholar who writes about prophecy

Colin and Becky Dial—Wisconsin couple with an underground hideout

Bo and Ginny Shairton, Maggie Carlson, Manny Aguilara—escapees from GC jail

Sam Goldberg—Jewish teenager, Lionel's good friend

Mr. Mitchell Stein—Jewish friend of the Young Trib Force

Chaim Rosenzweig—famous Israeli scientist

UNBELIEVERS

Nicolae Carpathia—leader of the Global Community

Leon Fortunato—Carpathia's right-hand man

Z-Van—lead singer for the popular group, The Four Horsemen

UNDECIDED

Claudia Zander—Morale Monitor, Natalie Bishop's former roommate

What's Gone On Before

JUDD Thompson Jr. and the others in the Young Tribulation Force are living the adventure of a lifetime. Still in Israel, Judd and Lionel Washington view a horrific plane crash, then find a ride to Jerusalem from a former terrorist.

As Vicki Byrne and her friends prepare to leave Iowa for Wisconsin, they discover their friend Pete Davidson has been captured by the Global Community. On the way, Vicki contacts an old friend, Josey Fogarty.

Chang Wong, a young believer working inside the Global Community in New Babylon, gives Judd the good news that the four believers on the plane are not dead. Instead, they are running Operation Eagle, a daring plan to save Israeli lives.

Vicki and the others return to Wisconsin after a dangerous getaway from GC forces in Illinois. There, they learn their friend Pete Davidson has died at the hands of the Global

Community. Still shaken by the news, the kids receive a cry for help from Morale Monitor Claudia Zander. After much discussion, Vicki, Mark, and their new friend Manny Aguilara rush to rescue her. On the way, they hear reports about a mysterious sickness breaking out around the world.

Thousands cheer the return of Nicolae Carpathia to Jerusalem as he rides a pig to mock Christ followers and Jews. The showdown begins between God's man "Micah" and Nicolae Carpathia. Lionel is horrified to see Nicolae commit murder in the temple.

Join the Young Tribulation Force as they try to survive the scariest events in the history of the world.

ONE

Innocent Blood

LIONEL Washington took a deep breath and tried to comfort his friend Sam Goldberg. They had just seen Nicolae Carpathia murder Sam's friend Daniel Yossef inside the temple.

Thousands had gathered to watch Nicolae's every move. Many supported him, flocking outside the temple like it was some sporting event. But Carpathia's words and actions repulsed followers of Jesus Christ and Orthodox Jews. Lionel had heard how cold-blooded Nicolae could be, but he never dreamed the man would kill in front of a live camera. Lionel couldn't understand why anyone would follow this evil man.

Sam looked at one of the huge television monitors and whispered, "Do you think Daniel believed the message about Christ before he was killed?"

"I hope so," Lionel said. "It took guts to refuse Carpathia's order to shoot at those Jewish leaders."

Lionel looked around for Judd. They had become separated earlier, and Lionel yearned for a familiar face. People trembled from the pain of sores breaking out all over their bodies. Many Morale Monitors and GC soldiers had moved to quickly constructed medical tents. Others without Carpathia's mark or the seal of God on their foreheads shook their fists and sprinted up the temple steps.

Through television monitors came the clear voice of God's prophet Dr. Chaim Rosenzweig, who called himself Micah. Somehow the Tribulation Force had broken into a live Global Community Network News feed, and this small, robed man was speaking out against the evil ruler.

"As Carpathia continues," Dr. Rosenzweig said, "you should be able to see the laver where the priests wash their hands before they approach the main altar. The temple was creatively placed over a series of underground waterways where gravity allows constant water pressure for the various cleansings. Of course, he has no business in this place, and even a ceremonial washing of his hands will not exonerate him for defiling it."

For some reason the camera switched back inside the temple, and the scene was so frightening Lionel turned away. Carpathia's eyes seemed to dance with glee as he stood over the dead man's body.

Sam gasped in disgust. "Look at his hands!"

Carpathia stared into the camera and held up two bloody hands. Someone inside the room said something and Carpathia sneered. "My faithful get the message." His voice echoed in the room as he shouted. "Any who dares interrupt my pilgrimage will find his blood on my fingers!"

*

Judd Thompson Jr. closed his eyes. Was this a bad dream or reality? As Chaim Rosenzweig tried to convince viewers around the world of Carpathia's evil, Mr. Stein drew close and tried to explain why the robed holy men would risk their lives to stop Nicolae. The priests scrambled up the stairs, yelling and shaking their fists. Judd glanced at the video monitor above him just as the camera whirled, the screen filling with priests charging like enraged animals.

"See where this blood comes from!" Carpathia shouted.

The priests stopped at the sight, their faces

pale. One at the front glanced at the body on the floor and threw out his arms. "Does your evil know no bounds?"

Nicolae's face reddened. "Are you the god-haters who do not know me as a god, a god acknowledged by all others, but not named by you?"

"It should not surprise you," one man said, "that we showed our loyalty by offering daily sacrifices on your behalf."

"You have made offerings," Carpathia spat, "but to another, even if it was for me. What good is it then, for you have not sacrificed to me? No sacrifice shall ever again be made in this temple except to me. Not *for* me, *to* me. Now leave or face the same fate as this unlucky one who was foolish enough not to believe that I have been allotted the nature of god!"

"God will judge you, evil one!"

"Give me your gun again, Supreme Commander!"

The priests took a step back, but one stood his ground. "We retreat not in fear but rather because you have turned the house of God into a killing field!"

Mr. Stein turned to Judd and whispered, "That is Ethan Ben-Eliezar. We have had many discussions about—"

Carpathia screamed again. "Just go! I shall have my way in my home, and should you

4

be found without proof of loyalty to me by week's end, you shall offer your heads as ransom."

The priests turned, shouting threats and joining their followers outside the temple. When the man Mr. Stein identified as Ethan Ben-Eliezar emerged, other priests cheered. He lifted both hands toward the sky and yelled, "Lovers of God, unite!"

The priests repeated the words until it became a chant. Judd glanced at the monitor again, expecting to see Carpathia mocking them, but Dr. Rosenzweig was back.

"The inner court inside the pillars has stairs that face east and lead to the main altar," Chaim began. "Priests who revere God march around the Court of Priests and the Holy Place with their left hands closest to the altar. This one who would trample holy ground has already begun the opposite way, so his right hand will be closest to the altar. The Scriptures foretold that he would have no regard for the one true God. What plans he has for the beast with which he ridiculed the Via Dolorosa will be revealed only as he invades deeper into God's own territory."

"He's going to do something with the pig he rode?" Judd said.

Mr. Stein pursed his lips.

Chaim continued, contrasting Carpathia's rantings with the way God had displayed his glory. "God appeared to Moses on Mount Sinai when the Ten Commandments were handed down. He appeared again when Moses dedicated the Tent of God. And finally he showed himself at the dedication of Solomon's Temple on this very site. Should God choose, he could reveal himself even today and crush under his foot this evil enemy. But he has an eternal plan, and Antichrist is merely a bit player. Though Antichrist has been granted power to work his horror throughout the world for a time, he shall come to a bitter end that has already been decided."

Vicki Byrne was riveted to the radio coverage from Israel. The news anchor explained that the audio was being taken from the video feed and broke in to talk over the man named Micah.

As Mark drove south, Manny Aguilara, the new believer who had escaped the Global Community, studied a map. Their plan was to rescue Morale Monitor Claudia Zander with the help of one of Manny's gang friends.

Between Carpathia's pig ride down the Via

Dolorosa and his assault on the temple, Manny told his story. Vicki was astounded when she heard how Manny had been placed in a cell next to Zeke Sr.

"Sure, I went to church with my mother when I was little. But when it came time to choose between the gang and God, the decision was simple. The gang gave me money, protection, and friends. It made sense to me back then."

"Did you ever try to get out?" Vicki said.

Manny shook his head. "I thought about it once or twice when things heated up. The police would get close or somebody would get shot and I'd wonder if it was worth it, but getting out is more dangerous than staying in."

"What do you mean?" Vicki said.

Manny pointed to a tattoo on his face, a small *x*. "I got this when I joined. Everyone knows you're part of the gang by this. They fear it. But try to leave, and your own gang wants you dead. Then other gangs come looking for you. It's easier and safer to stay in."

"Did anybody ever try to kill you?" Mark said.

Manny looked at the floor. "Our gang was into drugs. We had our territory and no one was supposed to cross the line. Our rivals violated the boundary, so our leader said I should go along to help end the problem."

"What do you mean, end the problem?" Vicki said.

"Usually you take a couple of guys and talk with the people, to scare them. But things had gone way past scaring. The disappearances changed everything. I don't know how to explain it, but we had lots more business and the violence was getting worse.

"The meeting with this rival turned ugly. Hector pulled his gun first, so it forced me to as well. Four people died that day."

There was silence in the car. Finally, Vicki said, "Four died because of a territory dispute?"

Manny nodded. "Sounds stupid now, but back then I dreamed about killing or being killed. Dying was just part of life."

"And you think one of these gang guys will help us?" Mark said.

Manny hesitated, then nodded. "The leader, Hector."

As they drove on, Vicki thanked God that Manny's life had changed. She knew they would be in great danger and was glad people were praying for them back in Wisconsin. The kids had set up a room where at least one person would be praying at all hours.

Now, listening to Carpathia on the radio and the voice of his right-hand man, Leon Fortunato, Vicki snapped back to reality. Leon had joined Carpathia in the temple and weakly said, "You, my lord, are the good spirit of the world and source of all good things."

※

Judd stayed close to Mr. Stein, asking questions when there was a lull in the action. He knew Carpathia wasn't finished defiling the temple, but he couldn't believe it could get worse.

"I don't understand how these people are going to get away from here," Judd whispered. "When is Operation Eagle going to begin?"

Mr. Stein looked concerned. "That is my question as well. We must take advantage of this window and put out a call to everyone to flee before Carpathia attacks."

Jewish priests filed by them, and Mr. Stein called out for Rabbi Ben-Eliezar. They were making such a commotion, still chanting, that the man didn't hear. Mr. Stein turned to Judd. "Stay here. I will talk with the rabbi and return."

Judd nodded, leaned against a stone, and surveyed the crowd. At times the noise was deafening, with Carpathia supporters trying to shout down the Orthodox Jews. Others who had taken the mark, Morale Monitors and soldiers, could barely stand. That seemed to give energy to the anti-Carpathia group, and they grew louder and more menacing as each minute passed.

Judd took a breath and prayed silently. "God, you know how much these people need to know you. You know how powerful the evil one is. I pray you would remove the blinders from those who haven't taken the mark yet. Help them see the truth about Jesus. And help us get out of here alive."

Lionel stayed with Sam as the crowd turned into a mob. There was so much noise around them—shouting, arguing, and people throwing dirt and stones—that the two had to huddle in a corner.

Sam finally stood, his face streaked with tears. "We'll never know if Daniel truly believed in God or not. Carpathia took his life in front of all these people and we're not doing anything."

Lionel put a hand on Sam's shoulder. "Calm down. We're going to get out of here."

"Is that what you want to do?" Sam said, pulling away. "You want to be safe?"

Sam suddenly glanced up. He whispered something under his breath as Lionel came out from behind their shelter and looked at the huge monitor nearby. Nicolae Carpathia approached a curtain that stretched out of the camera's view. Lionel noticed the crowd had quieted, mesmerized by what was on the screen.

"He's in the Holy of Holies," Sam whispered. "He's ready for the final defilement."

Carpathia grabbed the handle of a long knife he had tucked in his belt and dramatically raised it over his head. He reached as high as he could and plunged the gleaming steel through the veil. The fabric ripped as he pulled the blade all the way to the floor. Nicolae pushed each side of the curtain back, revealing the altar and the massive pig from the day before. There was no saddle this time. The pig struggled and tugged at ropes held by two men. Lionel wondered if this animal sensed evil.

Sam clenched his teeth. "I can watch this no longer. I have to do something!"

"Sam, wait!" Lionel said, trying to grab the boy's arm, but it was too late. Sam disappeared into the crowd of priests and Carpathia loyalists.

Vicki listened as the reporter in Jerusalem tried to describe the scene. Before he mentioned the pig, she heard it squeal in the background and guessed what was about to happen.

"Pull over right here," Manny said suddenly. He wiped his forehead with the back of his hand and squirmed in his seat.

"We're not that close, are we?" Mark said.

"Just pull over."

Mark parked on the darkened street and turned off his lights. Manny switched the radio off and sat back.

"What's the matter?" Vicki said.

"I didn't tell you the whole truth," Manny said. "In fact, I lied."

TWO

The Sacrifice

LIONEL raced into the crowd and caught up with Sam as the boy fell to the ground and buried his face in his hands. Lionel knelt beside him and put a hand on his shoulder.

"Look!" a man behind them shouted. "He's preparing the sacrifice!"

The holy men cried out, tearing their robes as Nicolae approached the huge pig. In the street, the animal had been slow and seemed drugged. Now it was thrashing around, squealing, and straining at the ropes. Two men struggled to hold it as Nicolae laughed. He jumped at the animal and slipped, the pig dodging him.

"Want to play?" Nicolae howled. Then he leapt onto the pig's back, sending the animal to its knees. For the next few seconds the pig tried to knock Nicolae off, but it was no use.

Finally, Carpathia plunged his knife into the animal's throat.

Nicolae fell to the ground, a flood of blood soaking his clothes. The pig went wild, thrashing and pulling its handlers. As the blood flow slowed, the pig fell and Nicolae cupped his hands under its neck. Lionel had to look away.

The crying and wailing of the holy men reached a crescendo and one priest screamed, "He has thrown the animal's blood on the altar!"

Lionel couldn't watch the gory scene that followed, but he could hear Nicolae trying to butcher the animal. Lionel turned to Sam. "Come with us. We're leaving soon."

"I must stay with my people," Sam whispered. "These men need to know that Jesus is the perfect sacrifice. How will they know if someone doesn't tell them?"

"I understand, but—"

More shouts from the crowd stopped Lionel. He stood for a better view of the screen. Nicolae had given the order to take the pig away and bring in his image. The holy men went berserk.

Carpathia washed off the blood and dried himself. Someone off camera handed him the shimmering white robe, silver sash, and gold sandals he had worn the day before. He put them on and looked at the camera. "Now, once my image is in place, we are out to Solomon's scaffold."

Suddenly the camera switched to a brown-robed man, shaking his head. The holy men around Lionel seemed hopeful again. Lionel studied the camera shot to try and figure out where Chaim Rosenzweig was, but the man's face filled the screen.

"Is this not the most vile man who ever lived?" Rosenzweig said. "Is he not the opposite of whom he claims to be? I call on all who have resisted or delayed in accepting his mark and plead with you to refuse it. Avoid the sentence of grievous sores and certain death."

❋

"What do you mean, you lied?" Vicki said.

Mark clenched his teeth. "This group is built on the trust of its members, and if you've—"

Manny held up a hand. "Let me explain."

"You've got thirty seconds," Mark said.

"What are you going to do, shove me out on the street?" Manny said. "Is that how you treat a fellow believer?"

"People who lie to us can't be part of the group," Mark said. "It's as simple as that."

"Just let him talk," Vicki said.

Manny sat back and took a deep breath. "When I spoke with Hector on the phone . . . I wasn't honest about what he said."

"You told us he would help us see if Claudia was legit," Mark said.

"You have to understand. My life has changed so much. When you helped me escape, I thought about all my friends who don't know God. That's everyone I know."

"What did you lie about?" Mark said.

"Hear me out," Manny said. "I was in jail because the Global Community knew I was involved with the shooting of those four people. They promised if I testified against Hector and a few others that I wouldn't see jail time."

"So you told them what they wanted to hear?" Vicki said.

"No. I didn't tell them anything. Maybe I should have. I don't know. I was more scared of Hector and the others than the GC. The point is, after I prayed and asked God into my life, I haven't been able to get Hector and the others out of my mind. Once we made it to Wisconsin, I figured I'd never have a chance to see the gang again."

"So you used this situation with Claudia to make contact," Mark said. "You've put us in danger."

"When you explained about this girl, I

thought it would be the perfect way to help you and reach out to my friends."

"What did Hector say when you called him?" Vicki said.

Manny frowned. "He didn't believe me. I told him I was free and he said it was a GC trick, that they were using me."

"Did you explain about Claudia?" Mark said.

"Hector blew up and said he would see me dead if I came back."

Mark rolled his eyes. "Great. Then why are we going there?"

"I know it sounds weird, but if I can see them one more time, I know I can get them to understand."

Vicki put a hand on Manny's shoulder. "We both understand how much you want to reach out to your old friends. All of us have felt that way."

"Yeah, but putting us in this situation isn't right," Mark said. "You could have the best intentions and go in there and—"

"I've been praying and asking God to get them ready," Manny interrupted. "I heard Dr. Ben-Judah or someone say that people's hearts will be hardened. I'm hoping I can get to the gang before any of them take Carpathia's mark."

"This throws everything off," Mark said. "How are we going to get to Claudia?"

"Please," Manny said, "take me to the gang. I'll go in alone. And I promise you, someone will help us."

***

Judd watched in horror as the angry mob reacted to Nicolae. The Temple Mount was near a riot with loyalists yelling support for the potentate and crying out in pain because of their sores. Christ followers and Orthodox Jews protested, while many undecided were caught up in the turmoil.

Judd wondered what it would take to convince the undecided about the potentate's identity. He had committed murder in front of the world and was acting like a wild man, calling for people to sacrifice offerings to him and saying the temple was his house.

Judd looked for Mr. Stein amid the group of priests but couldn't find him. Men with long beards fell to their knees, crying. "He would sacrifice a *pig* in the Holy of Holies and cavort in its blood?"

Another priest climbed to the top of the steps. "Those who live by the sword shall die by the sword! He has killed an innocent man in cold blood, and we demand his blood!"

A few men without Carpathia's mark came outside to move the golden statue. The holy men called for quiet as Nicolae's face appeared on-screen.

"Why worship at an altar of brass?" Nicolae sneered. "If this is indeed the holiest of holy places, every worshiper should enjoy the privilege of bowing to my image, which our Most High Reverend Father has imbued with the power to speak when I am not present!"

A murmur ran through the crowd, and Judd saw scores of priests running for the stairs. When the workers were ready to carry the golden Carpathia statue inside, a crowd surrounded them.

Mr. Stein rushed back to Judd's side. "I talked with Ethan briefly, and he said he would meet with me later if possible."

"Did you expect this?" Judd said, nodding to the ugly scene on the stairs.

Suddenly gunfire rang out and Judd hit the ground. Protesters surrounding the statue pulled back, cursing and waving their fists. The statue was moved inside to the Holy of Holies.

The human storm finally erupted. Morale Monitors and Peacekeepers, many too weak to lift a weapon, were attacked by the mob and trampled. A few managed to get off a shot or two, killing several protestors. Judd stayed down as a bullet struck a rock nearby. The shots sent the people into a frenzy. Medical tents fell, the guillotine was smashed to pieces, and GC vehicles turned on their sides. Several TV monitors crashed to the ground, scattering shards of glass.

"Kill Carpathia!" someone screamed.

"Death to the monster!" another said. "I hope he dies and stays dead!"

Judd noticed one TV monitor that hadn't toppled. Carpathia stepped back, his eyes wide. He said something Judd couldn't hear into the camera. Seconds later Mr. Stein pointed to the temple entrance where cabinet members, including Leon Fortunato, joined Carpathia. Rioters yelled.

Nicolae tried to speak, but the noise was too great. Finally, someone found a microphone that weakly amplified his voice through the remaining speakers in the outer court. Judd thought the man would try to soothe the people, but Nicolae raised a hand and said, "You have breached the covenant! My pledge of seven years of peace for Israel is rescinded! Now you must allow me and my—"

Thousands hollered, overwhelming the potentate's voice. Holy men pressed close to the temple entrance, keeping Carpathia and anyone else from exiting.

"You think Fortunato will call down fire like he did yesterday?" Judd said.

Mr. Stein pursed his lips. "I pray no more will die before they have a chance to hear God's man again."

Carpathia tried to capture his followers' attention. "My brothers and sisters of the Global Community! I will see that you are healed of your sores, and you will again see that it is I who love you and bring you peace!"

A young voice shouted, "You'll not leave here alive, pretender!" It was Sam, halfway up the steps of the temple.

The mob shook their fists and cheered, repeating Sam's words, laughing, screaming more death threats at Global Community leaders.

Leon Fortunato braced himself against a wall and said something to another GC cabinet member. Everyone behind Nicolae looked like they were at a funeral, and Judd wondered it if might be their own.

Piercing the din of the crowd came the voice of the man in the brown robe. Everyone hushed and remained riveted on him. "Yes," Mr. Stein said softly as Chaim began.

"It is not the due time for the man of sin to face judgment, though it is clear he has been revealed!" Dr. Rosenzweig said to the crowd. People murmured as Chaim walked through the main group of protestors. Out of respect, people took a step back as he ascended the temple steps. Judd thought it amazing that Nicolae had used a microphone and he could barely be heard, while Chaim spoke in a normal tone and everyone understood him.

"As was foretold centuries ago, God has chosen to allow this evil for a time, and impotent as this enemy of your souls may be today, much more evil will be perpetrated upon you under his hand. When he once again gains advantage, he will retaliate against this presumption on his authority, and you would do well to not be here when his anger is poured out."

Carpathia swung the microphone to his lips. "That is right! You will rue the day when you dared—"

"You!" Chaim roared and pointed at Nicolae. "You shall let God's chosen ones depart before his curse is lifted, lest you face a worse plague in its place."

"I have always been willing to listen to reasonable men," Carpathia said. "I will be at the Knesset,* available to negotiate or to answer honest inquiries from my subjects."

Judd stood, amazed, as the crowd parted

*Israel's Parliament

for Nicolae and his people. As they left, Chaim raised his arms and spoke. "Let those who are in Judea flee to the mountains. Let him who is on the housetop not go down to take anything out of his house. And let him who is in the field not go back to get his clothes."

"Why should we flee?" a man yelled. "We have exposed the potentate as an impotent pretender!"

"Because God has spoken!" Dr. Rosenzweig said.

"Now we're to believe *you* are God?" the man said.

"The great I Am has told me. Whatsoever he even thinks comes to pass, and as he purposes, so shall it stand."

"Praise God," Mr. Stein whispered. "Listen to the people. They are calm."

"Where shall we go?" someone asked.

"If you are a believer in Jesus Christ as Messiah," Chaim said, "leave now for Petra by way of Mizpe Ramon. If you have transportation, take as many with you as you can. Volunteers from around the globe are also here to transport you, and from Mizpe Ramon you will be helicoptered in to Petra. The weak, the elderly, the infirm, find your way to the Mount of Olives, and you will be flown in from there."

"And if we do not believe?"

Chaim paused. "If you have an ear to hear, make your way to Masada, where you will be free to worship God as you once did here at his temple. There I will present the case for Jesus as Messiah. Do not wait! Do not hesitate! Go now, everyone!"

THREE

Flashing Lights

WHILE Mark phoned their hideout in Wisconsin, Vicki talked with Manny. He apologized for his mistake and said he wouldn't blame them if they turned around and headed for safety.

"We decided a long time ago that we would do whatever we could to help people understand the message," Vicki said. "We want to stay away from Peacekeepers and Morale Monitors, but our first priority is reaching people with the truth."

Manny looked out the window. "I've been practicing what I'll say to Hector and the others. I'm not sure I can speak as well as you."

"You want me to go with you?"

"I couldn't ask that."

Mark hung up the cell phone. "Colin is ticked. He wants us to turn around."

Manny scratched his head. "Which one is Colin?"

"Colin Dial, the guy who owns the house where we're staying. He said we should get out of here and they'd figure out another way to help Claudia."

Manny sighed and reached for the door handle. "I guess this is where I get out."

"Stay where you are," Mark barked. "Some of the others were up and I talked to them on the speakerphone. They all thought after Claudia's latest e-mail that we should—"

"She wrote again?" Vicki said.

Mark nodded. "She said she's leaving her hotel by noon today and wants to know where she should go."

"Did they write back?"

"Yeah. They said they would send her instructions before noon."

"Good," Vicki said. "That makes it sound like we're going to send a message rather than show up."

"The kids voted to make Claudia our priority," Mark continued. "If we can help Manny meet with his friends and do it safely, they gave us the thumbs-up."

Manny smiled and glanced at Vicki. Suddenly his face contorted and he gasped.

"What is it?" Vicki said.

"GC squad car!"

Lionel moved along with Sam and the crowd making its way from the Temple Mount. He kept looking for Judd but couldn't find him. Many who had Carpathia's mark were trying to leave for Masada, and Lionel felt sorry for them. Though they didn't realize it, these people had decided their eternal fate when they had taken Nicolae's mark.

As they followed the crowd, Lionel turned to Sam. "You told me about Petra, but what's Masada?"

"It is an ancient site revered by the Jews," Sam said. "It looks like a huge boat in the middle of the desert."

"And it's made out of rock?"

"Exactly. In the first century, a Jewish uprising threw out the Romans who occupied the fort. Later, the Romans came back and attacked. After a long battle, the Jews realized they would be defeated, so they killed themselves rather than be captured by the Romans."

"Now I remember," Lionel said, still scanning the crowd for any sign of Judd. "What are you going to do?"

"I will eventually go to Petra, I think," Sam said, "but I have to go to Masada and see if I can help my fellow countrymen become followers of Messiah."

Lionel walked close to Sam, wishing he had stayed with Judd. Now there was no turning back.

🌟

Judd remained with Mr. Stein as the Temple Mount quickly emptied, leaving bodies, splintered wood, and trash. Judd even spotted a few Global Community issued handguns thrown on the ground.

Judd's cell phone rang.

"Where are you?" Chang Wong said.

Judd told him.

"I have just communicated to the rest of the Tribulation Force that I'll be able to let everyone hear exactly what happens between Carpathia and Dr. Rosenzweig at the Knesset."

"How did you manage that?" Judd said.

"Buck Williams is with Chaim and he's going to keep his cell phone on during the meeting. The sound won't be perfect, but we'll be able to hear most of what happens. Would you like to be included?"

"Yeah, but I don't have a computer right now—"

"That's okay. I'll patch your phone into the

system. I'll call when they arrive. Would you like to hear my good news?"

Mr. Stein motioned to Judd that he was going to speak with one of the rabbis and Judd nodded. "Sure."

"You know how concerned I was over my dual marks," Chang said. "When I heard there was a plague of boils, I even felt an itch on my leg and was afraid I was being affected. Now I know for sure what happened to me the morning I received Carpathia's mark."

Vicki whirled and noticed a GC squad car moving slowly toward them, less than a block away. Using its side-mounted search-light, it illuminated parked cars and checked license plates.

"Quick decision," Mark said. "Do we stay or risk pulling out?"

"It looks like a routine canvas," Manny said.

"But if we stay, they'll see us," Vicki said.

"Keep your lights off and ease out," Manny said. "Don't touch your brake or the lights will tip them off."

Mark started the car and slowly pulled forward, angling toward the street. Vicki rolled down her window slightly and studied the squad car behind them. "I don't think he's seen us yet," she said. Mark leaned over the steering wheel and peered into the dark.

"Another few blocks and I'll show you a place you can hide," Manny said.

Vicki heard a metal clinking and something darted across the road. "Mark, watch out!"

Mark slammed on the brakes, narrowly missing a small white dog that rushed in front of them. The dog scampered safely into the night, its tags tinkling as it ran.

"Move fast," Manny said. "They saw your brake lights."

The squad car turned its searchlight forward. Mark hit the accelerator and sped into the darkness, swerving wildly to miss a giant pothole. Flashing lights swirled and the car raced toward them, its siren blaring.

"Turn here!" Manny yelled.

Mark turned sharply and sped down a dark alley. "I have to turn on my lights!"

"Keep them off. I'll tell you where to go."

They passed a fenced-in area and several crumpled buildings. Vicki's heart raced as the squad car shot past the entrance to the alley. "They didn't see us turn!"

"Keep your lights off. They might be—"

The swirling lights returned as the squad car backed up and entered the alley.

"Turn left here," Manny said. "No brakes!"

Mark careened around the corner, barely missing a telephone pole and smashing into several trash cans. They were on gravel now, and the tires crunched bits of rock as they flew along the darkened side street. Manny leaned forward, struggling to see the next turn.

"They passed us again," Vicki said. "Wait, they're backing up!"

"Okay, a right turn coming up after an apartment building," Manny said. "Almost there, but we have to put some distance between us and them."

Mark pushed the car faster until Manny screamed. Mark had to hit the brakes and slid within a few inches of a concrete wall. A few yards more and they were back on a paved road. "Where are you taking us?"

"Just keep going," Manny said, looking behind them. "If they catch us, we'll lose our heads."

Mark strangled the steering wheel. "You two get out and hide, and I'll—"

"No, we're close," Manny said. "Keep going."

There were no working streetlights, and Vicki couldn't imagine how Mark drove without hitting something. The road was bumpy and at these speeds there was a chance of blowing a tire. Vicki closed her eyes and prayed. "God, help us get out of this without getting caught."

When she opened her eyes, the lights of the squad car seemed closer.

＊

Lionel followed Sam through the streets of Jerusalem. The uproar of the crowd at the Temple Mount continued as looters smashed windows and knocked over tables outside businesses. Outside bars, drunken men and women celebrated—though Lionel couldn't figure out why—by dancing and singing. Those who had Carpathia's mark soon fell behind, wailing in agony at sores that appeared on their feet.

Lionel saw one man shriek as he tried to wrestle a gun from an equally sick GC Morale Monitor.

"I can't go on like this!" the man screamed.

The Morale Monitor gained control of the weapon, took a step back, and aimed. "Stay where you are or I'll shoot!"

The man howled like a hurt animal and lunged wildly. The Morale Monitor fired, and the man crumpled to the ground. Lionel and Sam rushed over with several others. Someone rolled the man on his back, and blood poured from a wound in his chest. He gasped for air as his head lolled to one side. When he saw the Morale Monitor, he smiled slightly. "Thank you . . ."

One of the rabbis felt the man's neck and said he was dead. The Morale Monitor, who looked only slightly older than Lionel, seemed near hysterics. "I didn't have a choice! I told him to stop!"

Lionel and Sam left the group huddled around the man's body and kept following the crowd.

❄

Judd thought Chang sounded more excited than he had ever heard him. The young man had pieced together video and audio clips from secret recording devices planted throughout buildings in New Babylon.

"My father and Walter Moon gave me a tranquilizer," Chang said. "The drug made me forget the whole thing, including a conversation I had with my mother about being a believer."

"She's a believer?"

"Not yet, but she knows my sister, Ming Toy, and I are followers of Christ."

"That sounds like trouble. What if she tells your dad?"

"I'm praying both of them will see the truth before it's too late."

"What did you find out from the recordings?" Judd said.

Chang laughed with delight. "You don't know how relieved I was when I found video from a surveillance camera in one of the hallways. As my father and Walter Moon helped me walk—they pretty much carried me—I made the sign of the cross on my chest!"

"Incredible," Judd said.

"I don't even know where I got that! And then I pointed toward heaven and tried to say something."

"So it's clear you were resisting."

"Yes," Chang said. "God knew my heart and that they made me take the mark. Now I'm ready to do whatever I can to help the Tribulation Force."

Judd described the mayhem at the Temple Mount and asked Chang to call back when he had news from Carpathia's meeting at the Knesset.

"Watch for members of Operation Eagle," Chang said.

"How will I recognize them?"

"You'll know them when you see them."

Lionel became more concerned the farther he and Sam walked away from the Temple Mount. *Where are we going? How will we reach Judd?*

In the street ahead he noticed several parked vehicles. Men and women stood on top, waving and calling. These weren't Morale Monitors or Peacekeepers. They didn't wear uniforms and seemed too energetic.

As they drew closer, Lionel realized that all the people calling from the tops of their vehicles had the mark of the believer! Some yelled, "He is risen!"

Believers in the crowd answered, "Christ is risen indeed!"

Operation Eagle.

Vicki held on to the backseat as they drove across a deserted parking lot and into a run-down area. The GC squad car continued pursuit but seemed farther behind.

Manny grabbed the cell phone and punched a few numbers. He screamed something in Spanish and hung up.

"What was that about?" Mark said.

Manny ignored him and pointed Mark to a

battered brick building in the middle of the block. Mark pulled up to a garage door marked with graffiti, and Manny leaned over and gave the horn two short honks. The door opened and Mark drove inside. As soon as they stopped, the door banged shut behind them.

Seconds later Vicki heard the squad car siren approach.

FOUR

Knesset Conflict

VICKI held her breath. The only light in the garage came from the reflection of the red taillights, which cast an eerie glow about the room. Manny held up a hand for quiet and Mark turned. Vicki had been through many scrapes with Mark, but she had never seen him this frightened.

The siren grew louder, wailing and warbling, until it screamed outside the building. It surged, then quickly subsided as the car flew past the building.

"Stay where you are," Manny whispered. "We have to make sure they're not coming back."

The phone rang and Mark handed it to Manny. "It's for you."

Manny answered and listened. After a few moments he said something in Spanish, hung up, and turned to Mark and Vicki. "The squad car is gone, but I'm afraid we have another problem."

"Who were you talking to?" Vicki said.

"Hector. There's an observation room in the top floor—"

Before Manny could finish, a door opened and a shaft of light pierced the darkness. Vicki noticed a rickety staircase in front of them. A man stepped onto the landing above and pointed a gun. "Get out slowly," he said.

※

Lionel rushed to the waiting cars behind a wave of Orthodox Jews, who had neither the mark of Carpathia nor the mark of God. Operation Eagle members waved people farther back, filling up vans, cars, and trucks. One man had brought several ancient school buses, and people filled them in minutes.

"Lionel!" someone yelled from atop a Humvee ahead. At first, Lionel thought it might be Judd, but as he moved closer he saw Westin Jakes.

Westin jumped down and Lionel introduced Sam. Lionel explained that Westin was a pilot for the famous singer Z-Van and that he had flown Judd and Lionel to Israel.

Westin smiled. "Lionel is the one who

explained the truth to me after old Nicolae sat up in his glass coffin."

"What are you doing here?" Lionel said.

"Couldn't miss out on the excitement. I was at the airport, waiting for instructions from the boss, when I saw a lot of small plane activity. There were charters going out and some choppers, so I walked up to one of the guys doing his preflight and noticed he had the mark of the believer. He said he was with Operation Eagle. After he described it, I didn't have to think long. I knew I had to be part of it."

"What about Z-Van?" Lionel said.

Westin rolled his eyes. "I told you there would come a time when I'd have to stop working for him. I left a message at his hotel, but I haven't heard anything. I think he's brooding over the fact that he hasn't been able to perform his new material."

Lionel ran a hand along the Humvee. "Where'd you get this?"

"Airport rental." Westin winked. "I'm supposed to have it back the day after tomorrow, but I'm not sure where I'll be the day after tomorrow."

Lionel and Sam got in, and Westin fired up the big vehicle. "You guys can help. I'm supposed to find people who can't get

around very well and take them to the
Mount of Olives. Then it's off to Masada."

Sam spotted someone in a wheelchair and
Westin stopped. For the next few minutes
they picked up as many feeble or ailing
people as they could cram into the Humvee.

"Are you flying today?" Lionel asked.

Westin shook his head. "I'm only doing
ground transportation for now. This is one big
escape plan. The goal is to get as many people
out as we can before Carpathia attacks."

"Which way to Masada?" Lionel said.

"It's south toward En Gedi," Sam said,
"just a couple of miles off the western shore
of the Dead Sea."

"Where's Judd?" Westin said.

"Good question," Lionel said.

※

Judd watched the evacuation with a mixture
of delight and horror. From the frenzy
Carpathia had put the people in, Judd hadn't
expected anyone to leave. After all, the crowd
had Nicolae trapped. But something Dr.
Rosenzweig said—or maybe it was the way
he had said it—convinced people there was
real danger.

Judd and Mr. Stein followed one of the
Jewish leaders, Ethan Ben-Eliezar, to his

home. The rabbi tried to convince his wife to join the exodus.

"Why do we need to leave?" the woman said.

"We have been warned by a man who speaks with great authority. He may be a prophet of God."

"He's not a follower of Tsion Ben-Judah, is he?"

The rabbi glanced at Mr. Stein and Judd and took his wife by the arm. "We are only going to listen to what he has to say. It can't be any worse than what I just witnessed at the Temple Mount."

Judd wanted to find Lionel and Sam, but Mr. Stein insisted they keep moving. "I hope they have gone ahead to Petra. We will find them after we leave Masada."

※

Vicki shook as she slowly got out of the car with Mark and Manny. The three held up their hands and walked toward the stairs.

"Boss said he told you not to come here," the man with the gun said. "You must want to die."

"You didn't have to open the garage," Manny said.

The man squinted and stepped back,

making way. Manny led Mark and Vicki through a series of steel doors to a loft area. An old couch and several chairs had been thrown about the room. The wooden floor creaked when the three walked across it.

The man with the gun told them to sit. He glared at Manny. "Boss'll be down soon."

While they waited, Manny told them more about how he had gotten involved with the gang, the regular payoffs to GC authorities, friends who had died, and how his mother had reacted to his gang involvement.

"I kept it a secret from her for a long time, but she finally found out. She had talked about me going to live with relatives, and I found a letter from an uncle in Georgia saying he would take me in, no questions."

"Why didn't he?" Vicki said.

"That's when everybody disappeared. My mom was gone, and for all I know, my uncle too. I decided to move in here."

"How did you know they'd open the garage when you called?" Mark said.

"I gave them the signal and hoped. There's somebody up all the time, waiting for anybody in trouble." Manny rubbed his hands and looked at the floor. "I know you wanted to focus on getting Claudia out, but I figured this was our only shot to get away from the GC."

"Do they let people come in here who aren't part of the gang?" Vicki said.

"I've only seen it happen a couple of times, and the people they brought here didn't make it out alive."

✳

Judd squeezed into the backseat of Rabbi Ben-Eliezar's car with Mr. Stein. As the rabbi drove, he described to his wife what had happened at the Temple Mount and the awful display of Nicolae Carpathia.

Mrs. Ben-Eliezar put a hand to her head and gasped.

Judd's phone rang and Chang talked quickly. "You'll just get the raw feed from the Knesset. I won't be able to explain who's talking or what's going on, okay?"

"Got it."

The phone line crackled, and Judd heard groaning in the background. He had always had a good ear for voices, being able to identify people after only a few words on the phone.

Nicolae Carpathia said, "Forgive me for not standing."

"I represent the one true God and his Son, Jesus, the Christ," Dr. Rosenzweig said. "I prefer to stand."

After a moment, Nicolae said, "All right." The man seemed furious. "I am letting these people run off to the hills. When do the sores go away? I upheld my end of the bargain."

"We had a bargain?" Dr. Rosenzweig said. Judd pictured him in his brown robe, standing up to the most powerful ruler in the world.

"Come, come! We are wasting time!" Carpathia sneered. "You said you would lift this spell if I—"

"That is not my recollection. I said that if you did *not* let them go, you would suffer yet a worse plague."

"So I let them go. Now you—"

"It is not as if you had a choice."

Something banged on the table and Carpathia screamed, "Are we here to play word games? I want the sores on my people healed! What do I have to do?"

"Make no attempt to stop Israeli Messianic believers from getting to Petra."

Carpathia paused. Judd wondered how many of his top cabinet members were in the room, suffering from sores. "Have you not noticed? I am the only full-time employee of the Global Community not suffering from the plague!"

"And that only because you have not taken

your own mark, though I daresay you worship yourself."

Footsteps. Nicolae came close to the phone. "Our medical experts have determined there is no connection between the application of the mark of loyalty and—"

"Why does your bad breath not surprise me?"

Judd laughed.

"You do not dare to lift the curse for fear your fate will be the same as that of your two associates at the Wall."

"If your medical experts know so much, how is it that they have been able to offer no relief?"

"What is going on?" Mr. Stein said.

Judd put a finger to his lips. "I'll tell you as soon as the meeting's over."

Carpathia had just finished asking a question when Judd put the phone to his ear again. Dr. Rosenzweig said, "I am here to remind you that this script has already been written. I have read it. You lose."

"If I am not god," Carpathia said, "I challenge yours to slay me now. I spit in his face and call him a weakling. If I remain alive for ten more seconds, he, and you, are frauds."

Judd shook his head. He wished God would take Nicolae up on his challenge.

"What kind of a God would he be if he felt compelled to act on your timetable?" Dr. Rosenzweig said, a smile in his voice.

Something happened in the background. Carpathia was talking with others in the room. Finally, Nicolae said, "My people are pleading for respite. I recognize that I am forced to concede something."

"And that would be?"

"That . . . I . . . must . . . submit to you in this. I am prepared to do what I have to do to enable a lifting of the plague."

Dr. Rosenzweig spoke slowly and firmly. "You are under the authority of the God of Abraham, Isaac, and Jacob, maker of heaven and earth. You will allow this exodus, and when I am satisfied that the people under my charge are safe, I will pray God to lift the affliction."

"How long?" Nicolae said.

"This is a huge undertaking. Six hours should be telling. But should you attempt to lay a hand on one of the chosen, the second judgment will rain down."

"Understood," Carpathia said quickly.

There was movement in the room, and Judd assumed Buck and Dr. Rosenzweig were leaving. Before Judd turned off the phone, Carpathia growled, "Your days are numbered."

Judd put the phone down, his hands shaking. He had seen Carpathia's evil display, but he had never heard his voice so close.

Judd told the others what he had heard and Rabbi Ben-Eliezar asked how he had access to such a meeting. Without giving away anyone's identity, Judd explained that the Tribulation Force had contacts throughout the Global Community.

"It is our desire to convince as many people as possible of the true identity of Nicolae Carpathia," Mr. Stein said, "and the identity of Carpathia's heavenly foe."

"Who is that?" Mrs. Ben-Eliezar said.

⁂

Vicki watched the seconds tick by on a digital clock. Finally, a door opened and a heavy-set man with a mustache walked into the loft.

Manny stood and the man waved at him to remain seated. "Hector, I'm sorry—"

"You must not have understood me on the phone. Did you bring the GC or just these two?"

"Please let me explain."

Hector looked out a window behind Vicki. A pink strip of light shone on the horizon. "I'll give you until I can see the sun peek over those buildings, which won't be long."

Vicki glanced at Mark, who had his eyes closed. She hoped the kids in Wisconsin were still praying.

FIVE

Off to Masada

JUDD listened as Mr. Stein explained from both the Old and New Testaments what he believed about Nicolae Carpathia. Mrs. Ben-Eliezar listened with interest as the rabbi drove silently. When he had talked for many miles, Mr. Stein switched the conversation to Mrs. Ben-Eliezar and asked about her family.

"We have two grown boys. One is in Haifa, the other in Tel Aviv. Things have been very hard, but they come to see us as often as they can. We had a girl. . . ." The woman glanced at her husband.

Mr. Stein sat forward. "What happened to her?"

Mrs. Ben-Eliezar clutched a tissue, as if she knew she was going to need it. "She went to America a few years ago to study. Anyway, she passed away."

"Was she part of the disappearances?"

"We should not talk of this," the rabbi said.

Mrs. Ben-Eliezar turned, tears in her eyes, and nodded.

"Let me guess," Mr. Stein said. "At the university, she met some religious fanatics. Maybe had one for a roommate. And they convinced her to turn her back on her beliefs. It broke your heart."

The woman hung on every word, wiping away tears. She looked at her husband. "Did you tell him?"

"I've heard this story before," Mr. Stein said. "My own daughter, Chaya, was also taken in by the message your daughter—"

"Meira was my daughter's name," Mrs. Ben-Eliezar interrupted.

"—yes, Meira. She no doubt tried to convince you that the Messiah had already come."

"She wrote letters, called, even made a special trip home from school. We were all heartbroken."

"When Chaya talked to my wife and me, I was so upset that I turned my back on her." Mr. Stein's lip quivered. "I considered her already dead, told my wife that she was to no longer speak Chaya's name in our home."

Judd noticed the rabbi had gripped the steering wheel tighter.

"Did your daughter disappear?" Mrs. Ben-Eliezar said.

Mr. Stein told Chaya's story, how she had heard of Messiah after the vanishings and had convinced her mother that Jesus had come back for his own. "Chaya died during the great earthquake."

"I'm sorry," Mrs. Ben-Eliezar said. "Meira went back to the States and only a short while later came the worldwide disappearances. We received word from the school that her things were found in her dorm room, but she was gone." The woman put her head in her hands and her shoulders shook. "I have heard all the theories. Do you have an explanation?"

Mr. Stein put a hand on her shoulder. "Yes, I know exactly what happened to your daughter, and I have good news."

"You do?"

"I believe you and your husband can see her again."

———— ✦ ————

Vicki sat perfectly still, silently praying for her new friend. Manny told Hector about his interrogation by the Global Community and what they had promised if he testified.

Hector sipped coffee and listened. When Manny described his escape from the GC jail, Hector looked at Vicki. "Why would you risk going to jail for someone like him? Do you know what he would do to you if he had the chance?"

"Manny is our brother now," Vicki said. "We couldn't leave him behind."

Hector gently placed his mug on a wooden table. "What if your brother is a murderer?"

"He's told us about the things he's done. He's changed."

Hector sat back and folded his arms. "And what brought about this *change?*"

"Did you hear about the man who chose to take the blade instead of Carpathia's mark?" Manny said.

Hector nodded. "The fool. It's just a little tattoo, nothing to worry about."

"Whatever you do, don't take that mark," Manny said. "It will seal your destiny forever."

The man holding the gun in the corner laughed and Hector joined in. "Did you get religion in that jailhouse?" Hector said. "Is that why you want me to trust you and help you with some Morale Monitor whose soul you're also trying to save?"

"What I heard in prison made me want to

risk my life and come here to tell you the truth."

Vicki glanced over her shoulder. The sun was an orange ball peeking over the horizon. Hector seemed intrigued. "So if I search you three, I won't find a recording device or a locator. The GC aren't going to be bursting in with guns blazing?"

Manny stood and pulled up his shirt. "Search all of us. I swear to you, we're not working with the GC."

Hector rose and turned to the man with the gun. "Make sure they're clean and get them something to eat."

"Don't you want to hear what I have to say?" Manny said.

"Get something to eat. I'll be back."

❋

Lionel watched eagerly as Westin took a small road through the Dung Gate and headed for the Mount of Olives. Two of their passengers were believers going to Petra, the rest to Masada. People streamed past, heading for the Mount, passing ancient trees and historical sites along the winding road. Westin drove around the Kidron Valley and pulled as far up on the Mount as he could.

Lionel and Sam got out to help two elderly

believers climb the rest of the way to the shuttle area. The view took Lionel's breath away. From here, he could see a panorama of the Old City of Jerusalem, the walls, the new temple, and a line of thousands moving into place on the Mount.

Operation Eagle volunteers greeted people and gave them instructions. "Helicopters will move into position here within a few minutes," one man said through a bullhorn. "Be patient with us as we try to go as quickly as we can."

"How long do you think it will take to move this many people?" Sam said.

"Depends on how many choppers they have lined up," Westin said. "Let's go."

They hopped back in the Hummer, headed toward Masada, and picked up three more passengers who had mistakenly come to the Mount of Olives.

Westin's phone rang and he looked at the readout. "Brace yourself—it's him." He turned the speaker on and answered.

Z-Van yelled a string of profanities at Westin. When the man took a breath, Westin interrupted. "I take it you're not happy with me."

Z-Van groaned, clearly in pain. "Get back here right now! We're playing tomorrow for the potentate's celebration. I want you ready to leave when we're done."

"I don't think you should plan anything with the potentate right now," Westin said. "From the amount of people I see leaving Jerusalem, he's going to have his hands full the next few days."

"When I want your opinion, I'll ask. I want you to make sure the plane's ready."

"With all due respect, you sound awful," Westin said. "How are you going to perform with sores all over your body?"

"How did you know I had sores?"

"Lucky guess."

"It doesn't matter. The potentate assured me personally that the problem would be gone within a few hours."

"How can he do that?" Sam whispered.

Lionel shrugged as Z-Van ordered Westin to return to the airport.

"No can do, sir. I'm driving some people to Masada. You can probably hire a pilot for a lot less than you pay me."

Z-Van cursed again. "I've paid you to do a job. You're under contract! I can sue you for everything you're worth."

"Which is not much, sir. I think it's time we go our separate ways."

"I'll decide when that is," Z-Van screamed.

"Just finish whatever you're doing and get back here, understand?"

"I'll check back after my trip."

Click.

"You could have just told him you were a believer now," Sam said.

Westin smiled. "Want to hear my wild dream?"

"What?" Lionel said.

"We wind up using Z-Van's plane for believers."

＊

As they drove south, Judd listened to Mr. Stein explain the truth about the disappearances to Rabbi Ben-Eliezar and his wife.

After a few minutes of conversation, the rabbi asked him to stop. "You're asking me to do the same thing my daughter wanted me to do."

"If you put your hope and trust in Christ, you will see your daughter again."

"We may not survive the night," the rabbi said. "You expect me to believe that Carpathia will live up to another agreement?"

"Carpathia is a liar at heart," Mr. Stein said. "You cannot trust anything he says. Besides, I already know he is going to break his agreement."

Mrs. Ben-Eliezar turned. "How could you know that?"

"This is from careful reading of Revelation, chapter 12. Tsion Ben-Judah agrees. In that chapter we are told that Israel will be given two wings like those of a great eagle. Israel flies to a place prepared for her in the wilderness. She will be cared for and protected there."

"But what makes you think Carpathia will attack?" the rabbi said.

"It says the dragon will try to drown Israel with a flood that comes from the dragon's mouth. Dr. Ben-Judah believes this flood refers to the Antichrist's army."

"Oh dear," Mrs. Ben-Eliezar said.

"But the Scripture goes on to say that the earth will help Israel by opening its mouth and swallowing the river that gushes from the dragon's mouth."

"What could that mean?" the rabbi said.

"I don't know exactly, but as the Lord has shown himself faithful in the past, I believe it means he will somehow overcome this military operation."

Judd checked his watch. If he was right, the plague of boils would end at about nine that evening. Would Carpathia test God again?

He phoned Chang and thought he heard Nicolae's voice in the background.

"Hang on," Chang said, putting down the phone. When he came back on the line, he said, "I've just heard a conversation between Sick Nic and his top people."

"Sick Nic?"

"If I had time to play this back, you'd understand. It gave me major goose bumps. Where are you?"

"Headed toward Masada. Lionel and I got separated, so—"

"You may want to rethink that."

"Why? What did Carpathia say?"

"It's not only what he said, but what he did. You were at the Temple Mount when the head of the Morale Monitors tried to kill Dr. Rosenzweig, right?"

"Yeah, Loren Hut."

"Right. He's dead."

Judd gasped. "What happened?"

"Hut talked back to Carpathia, was sarcastic, and Nicolae shot him."

Judd shook his head. "Carpathia's out of control."

"He sure is. And he says once the curse is lifted, his enemies will be bunched up in four places or in the air."

"Mount of Olives, Masada, Mizpe Ramon, or Petra."

"Exactly, and he's declared all of Israel a no-fly zone at 9:15."

"There could still be planes and helicopters in flight."

"And my guess is, the GC will try to shoot them down. They're also planning an attack on Masada at 9:30."

"What?" Judd said.

"Carpathia wants to wipe out the Orthodox Jews and the Judah-ites wherever they are."

"Then everybody needs to head to Petra," Judd said.

Mr. Stein asked what was happening and Judd held up a hand.

"Carpathia says Petra is just as defenseless against their weapons as Masada," Chang said. "Judd, if God doesn't do something miraculous, you guys could all die out there tonight."

SIX

Manny's Decision

VICKI ate some fruit and toast and tried to
fight fatigue. She didn't know how long she
had been up or how long she had been
running on adrenaline. It had to catch up
soon, but she reminded herself of their
mission. Claudia Zander was out there,
running from the GC, and needed help. At
least, that's what she said.

Vicki drank coffee and winced. It perked
her up a little but left a bad taste. Another
gang member walked into the garage and
came out a few minutes later and spoke to
the man with the gun.

"What do we do about Claudia?" Vicki
said.

"If they let us go," Mark said, "I say we go
get her."

Vicki put the cell phone in her lap and

redialed the Wisconsin hideout. Darrion answered and sounded like she had been asleep. Vicki spoke softly and told Darrion what had happened. "Have we gotten any more messages from Claudia?"

"I'll check," Darrion said. The girl asked someone to wake up. *Probably Janie*, Vicki thought.

"Okay, it looks like a message came in from her a few minutes ago."

"Read it."

" 'Dear Young Trib Force, it looks like time is running out. I don't think I can wait much longer. Please tell me if you're coming or not. Claudia.' "

The man with the gun stirred, walking closer.

"Write her back and tell her—"

"Hey, no phone calls!" the man yelled.

"—to stay where she is. We'll be at her place as soon as we can get there."

"I said, no phone calls!" the man said, grabbing the phone and turning it off.

"She's not calling the GC," Manny said.

"Shut up, traitor!"

Manny stood, eyes flashing. "I'm a traitor? I'd like to see how long you would last in a GC jail cell, Carlos. How long would you hold out until you squealed on your friends and turned them in?"

"I know one thing," Carlos answered. "I wouldn't use religion as a crutch."

Manny shook his head. He was about to say something when a door opened and a young woman walked in.

Carlos smiled. "Now let's see what a tough guy you are."

The girl was dressed in a jogging suit and wore a scarf over her brown hair. Her brown eyes locked on Manny as she marched across the room. She stopped inches from his face and stared.

Before Manny could speak, the girl slapped him hard. The blow left a handprint on his face. He turned his head slightly, then looked into her eyes.

The girl clenched her teeth. "That was for getting caught!" She swung again. "And this is for leaving me alone!"

Manny caught her right hand in midair. She swung the other and he blocked it. They stood facing each other until the girl's shoulders shook. Manny let go of her arms, and the girl hugged him tightly and wept. "I thought you were dead."

Mark whispered to Vicki, "Looks like he had more people to talk with than Hector."

"Anita," Manny said, "I told you to leave and go to—"

The girl put a hand over his mouth and shook her head. "I couldn't leave. I knew you'd find a way to get back."

"I'm sorry you got involved in this. Have they taken care of you?"

The girl nodded. "Hector brought me here soon after you were arrested." Manny grabbed her shoulders and Anita smiled. "They haven't hurt me."

A wave of relief showed on Manny's face. He turned to Vicki and Mark. "I want you to meet my new friends." He put his arm around the girl and kissed her cheek. "This is my sister, Anita."

❋

Lionel marveled at the Hummer's electronic navigation system. He had used global positioning devices before—his mom and dad had both had one—but this one included a computer screen with 3-D images of what was ahead and behind them on the road, their speed, distance to their destination, and a projected arrival time.

"Will that thing tell us if the GC are going to attack?" Lionel smirked.

Westin touched a button on the screen. "Watch this."

A number flashed at the top indicating the

current temperature. The readout also included wind velocity, barometric pressure, and humidity. As the statistics flashed on the screen, the 3-D image tilted skyward, revealing a gridded outline of the sky. "I've got it on ten miles right now, but you can set it for twenty, fifty, a hundred, or more."

"What's it do?" Sam said.

"Lets you know about aircraft activity," Westin said. "Some use it to avoid radar detection from choppers. It could also be used in a military situation. These rigs are usually decked out with lots of gizmos people never use."

"Can you set it to look back at the Mount of Olives?" Lionel said.

Westin touched the screen a few more times and the grid enlarged. He pointed to the left side of the screen. "I could put in the coordinates, but this is basically the location of Jerusalem—here. The Mount of Olives is about here."

"What are all those dots to the right?" Sam said.

Lionel leaned closer and smiled. "Operation Eagle!"

Judd told Mr. Stein what Chang had said about Carpathia's plans. As he described the situation, Judd saw fear on the faces of Rabbi Ben-Eliezar and his wife.

"I think we should continue to Masada," Mr. Stein said. "The prophet God has sent told us to—"

"Your prophet told you to go toward Petra," Rabbi Ben-Eliezar said. "Only people like us should go to Masada, right?"

Mr. Stein rubbed his forehead. "True. But I feel called to Masada to help unbelievers in any way I can."

"Is that what we are to you?" Mrs. Ben-Eliezar said.

Mr. Stein leaned close. "I don't mean to offend you with my words about the Messiah. You have a knowledge of God and a zeal for him." He looked at Rabbi Ben-Eliezar. "You risked your life because you love God's house and didn't want to see it defiled. But God is asking you not just to be zealous for him, but to know his Son. He sent Jesus as the perfect sacrifice for sins so that—"

"Enough," the rabbi said. "I know your position."

"Please do not harden your heart," Mr. Stein said. "God has given you an opportunity to know him fully, through Jesus."

The line of vehicles stretched for miles

toward Masada. Judd phoned Chang again but his line was busy. He wondered what new plans Chang might uncover that could help believers in the coming days.

Judd sat back and prayed that Lionel and Sam would find a way to the safety of Petra—if Petra truly was safe. Would God's protection extend to all believers, or was it only for those who were Jewish?

Judd watched the terrain change as they drove closer to Masada. He thought of others in the Young Trib Force and prayed for their safety. When he thought of Vicki, he felt a strange ache. He believed his time spent in Israel and the Middle East was something only God could orchestrate, but he longed for home, to see his friends, and especially Vicki. So much had happened since he had last seen her. Maybe he wouldn't make it back to the States at all. Perhaps the next few days would decide that.

Still, Judd held out hope that he would return one day soon and put his troubles with Vicki behind him. Judd laid his head against the door and closed his eyes. Though there was much to fear, he knew the best and safest place to be was where God wanted him.

"I'm yours, God," Judd prayed. "I'll do whatever you want."

Vicki listened as Manny told Anita how the Global Community had caught him and what had happened in jail. When he described his conversation with Zeke, Anita looked away.

"I've heard of jailhouse conversions, but I never thought you'd be one of them," Anita said.

"Me either. But I've wanted to find you and tell you since it happened. You have to listen."

Vicki turned as Hector approached Manny. "No bugs in the car. Your story checks out. Our guy close to the GC says they're still looking for you. Go."

Vicki and Mark stood. Manny looked at them, then at Hector. "I'd like your permission to stay."

"Why?"

Manny took a breath. "I could leave here right now and do lots of good things with my life. I could tell other people I meet what has happened to me and what a change I've experienced, and maybe it would help them. But I've been thinking that I was given this gift so I could give it to the people I care about most."

Hector smiled. "You want to be a preacher

to the gangs? You think you'll get brownie points in heaven?"

Manny looked at Vicki and Mark again. "I know how much these people did for me, and they didn't even know me. How much more should I care about the only family I have left? How could I live with myself if I kept life from you? The stinging locusts, the earthquake, everything we've seen the last few years has a purpose, and it's to get our attention. Let me stay and tell you."

"Keep your religion," Hector said. "It would spoil our business."

Manny walked closer. "If you harden your heart against God, you will never know true freedom."

Hector shook his head. "Freedom? The only freedom I need is from nuts like you. Stay if you want, but you'll obey orders like before." He walked out of the room.

Mark put a hand on Manny's shoulder. "This is suicide. If you don't get out—"

"I know," Manny interrupted. "I think this is where I'm supposed to be."

Vicki looked at Mark. She knew Manny had made up his mind. "If you need help, you know how to reach us. We'll do all we can."

"Take this," Mark said, handing his watch to Manny. He showed him how to work The

Cube, a high-tech, 3-D demonstration of the gospel.

Manny looked at Vicki and Mark through tears. "What would I have done? Where would I be today, if you had not helped me?"

"Be faithful with the message," Vicki said. "God put you here for a reason."

"But what about Claudia?" Manny said.

Vicki shook her head. "Stay. We'll sort that out."

"Vicki's right," Mark said. "This may be your only chance to talk with your sister and the others."

Manny gave specific directions to Claudia's hotel and retrieved their cell phone. Manny led them to the garage and Vicki waved as they pulled away.

Vicki sighed. "What now?"

"We have two options," Mark said. "Head back to Wisconsin or go after her."

"We haven't come this far to turn back," Vicki said.

Colin Dial answered when Vicki called the Wisconsin safe house. "Darrion sent your message, and Claudia said she was still at the hotel. Room 223. What's going on down there?"

Vicki quickly explained how they had eluded the GC and that Manny had chosen to stay with the gang. As she talked, Vicki kept an eye out for any GC squad cars. Mark spotted one coming the other way and calmly kept driving. The officers seemed not to notice them.

A few minutes later, Mark pulled into a parking lot a block from the hotel. He got the phone number from a sign on the side of the building advertising weekly rates and told the desk worker he was looking for a safe place to have a family reunion.

After a few minutes he hung up. "She said there hasn't been any GC activity there that she knows of, so our reunion looks like a go."

Vicki shook her head. "You know I don't like it when you lie to people."

"Sorry. I thought it would help to know if—"

Vicki held up a hand and looked at her watch. They had plenty of time to find Claudia and leave.

Mark unbuckled and opened the door.

"You're not going without me," Vicki said.

"They'll recognize your face."

Vicki pulled out a hat Manny had given her and pushed her hair underneath. She put on bright red lipstick and a pair of sunglasses. "Let's go."

Mark shook his head. "Okay, but follow my lead."

Mark and Vicki stole through an alley and around a concrete barrier to the street. They crossed a half block from the hotel and worked their way back, keeping a close watch for any GC vehicles. The hotel rose six stories and Vicki kept an eye on the windows for anyone watching.

Several people sat in the lobby eating breakfast when Vicki and Mark walked inside. Vicki's heart beat faster as they approached the front desk. She saw a surveillance camera in the corner so she picked up a newspaper and pretended to read while Mark approached a woman clicking at a computer screen.

"I called a few minutes ago about a family reunion," Mark said.

"Yes?" the woman said, not looking up.

"Would it be possible for my sister and me to look at one of your rooms?"

"How many in your party?"

"We'd probably be renting a whole floor."

The woman looked up. "Most rooms have two double beds. A few have king-size with whirlpool baths."

"And meeting rooms?" Mark said. "How many will those hold?"

"Up to two hundred," the woman said. "You'll have to make food arrangements outside. We don't provide that."

"Of course," Mark said. He studied a layout

of the building as the woman grabbed a key. "Could we see something close to the pool? I think that's on the second floor, isn't it?"

The woman nodded. "Yes, if you'll let me see some identification, you can go right up."

Mark dug out the fake ID Colin Dial had helped him create and handed it to her.

She wrote down the information and gave him a card. "Room 264 is down the hall and around the corner from the pool, but that's the closest I could find that's clean. Take the elevator across the hall or the stairs down there."

"Great," Mark said. "We'll be right back."

Vicki followed Mark to the stairs. He paused and held the door slightly open.

"What?" Vicki said.

"I want to make sure that woman's not calling anybody."

He finally closed the door and they ran to the second floor and opened the door quietly. A soda machine hummed around the corner. Room 201 was directly across the hall.

"You ready?" Mark said.

"Yeah, let's go."

SEVEN

How Sweet the Sound

VICKI followed Mark into the hallway, and a wave of chlorine assaulted her senses. Before her sister, Jeanni, had been born, Vicki's family spent a couple of weekends every year at what her dad called "a fancy hotel." Vicki spent hours at the pool with her older brother, Eddie, ate at nearby restaurants, and once she remembered getting room service.

The door to the pool opened and Vicki heard splashing. She missed the laughs and giggles of kids around a pool, of kids in general. An older woman carried a bucket of ice inside and closed the door.

"Her room is right up there," Mark whispered. "Play it cool when we go by. Don't stare."

They walked confidently down the hall. 215. 217. 219. Vicki slowed a little and listened for a television, someone talking, perhaps a GC radio. They passed 221. Mark squeezed by a laundry cart ahead, and Vicki paused as she passed 223. A maid across the hall loaded wet towels into a basket. Covers and sheets lay strewn on the floor.

A door opened suddenly behind her and Vicki nearly screamed.

"Excuse me," a man said loudly.

Vicki stopped, took a breath, and turned. She expected a Peacekeeper or Morale Monitor, but instead saw a man in his undershirt, his hair neatly combed back and parted in the middle, hands on hips. "I called down to the front desk twenty minutes ago and asked about an ironing board!"

The maid walked into the hallway. "Very sorry, sir," she said in broken English. "I . . . get now." The woman hurried to the elevator as Vicki followed Mark to 264. He had the door open when she got there.

"It's going to take that cleaning woman a few minutes to get back," Vicki whispered. "Let's go into the room that's being cleaned."

Vicki led the way back down the hall and slipped into room 224. Mark closed the door behind him and watched the hallway through the tiny hole in the door. "Call her."

Vicki scanned the directions and figured out how to dial the room directly. As she was about to punch in the final number Mark put up a hand. "Hang on, somebody's coming."

"Is it Claudia?"

"Only if she's six feet tall and has a mustache. Okay, he's going into that guy's room. Go ahead."

Vicki dialed 2-2-3 and heard a faint ringing through the door. Someone answered on the second ring.

"Claudia?" Vicki said.

"Who is this?" a girl said.

"Claudia, if this is you, please—"

"Vicki? I hope you're not anywhere near here."

"Why? What's wrong?"

"A GC cruiser just pulled up in front of the hotel. I think somebody saw my picture and identified me. Are you outside?"

"We're close," Vicki said.

"We? You shouldn't have risked bringing anybody else. But I'm glad you're here."

"We need to get you out," Vicki said. "What's the best way?"

"The back of the hotel! I'll take the stairs and meet you there."

A knock outside. "Housekeeping!"

"Cleaning woman's back with the ironing board," Mark whispered.

"Wait a minute," Claudia said. "Are you guys in the hotel?"

The door slammed across the hall. "Go toward the back and we'll meet you," Vicki said. She hung up as the maid put her key card in the door.

Mark opened it and the woman jumped back. "Sorry," he said, holding up both hands.

Vicki and Mark scooted past her as the door to room 223 opened. Vicki glanced at a tall, blonde girl and recognized Claudia from her picture on TV. Vicki stared at the girl's forehead where she expected to see the mark of the believer.

Nothing.

"I told you they'd come!" Claudia yelled into a radio. "Where are you guys? There's two of them! One male, one female!"

"Run!" Mark yelled, shoving the heavy laundry cart to block the hallway.

"You'll wind up just like Bishop, with your head in a basket!" Claudia shouted. She tried to get around the cart as Mark and Vicki sped down the hall. "They're heading away from the pool on the second floor. Somebody watch the exits!"

Vicki turned the corner with Mark not far behind. Claudia cursed and screamed at the maid. "Get this out of my way!"

Footsteps pounded up the back staircase as Vicki put the key card into the door of room 264. Mark ducked in behind her and closed it quickly. The two struggled for breath and listened as someone ran past, wheezing and groaning.

"Where are they?" Claudia demanded. "You're moving so slow!"

"They didn't come out the southeast stairs!" a young man said. "And take it easy, you don't have sores all over—"

"Quit making excuses!" Claudia sighed and moved down the hall. "I told those guys to give me another hour!" She clicked her radio and gave the name of the hotel. "We have two Judah-ites cornered and need some help!"

Vicki closed her eyes and whispered, "The whole thing was a setup. That commander guy on TV set the trap and Claudia lured us here."

"We have to find a way out," Mark said. He rushed to the window and peeked through the curtains. "No GC cars out front. Sounds like they thought we weren't coming, so we might have a chance if we hurry."

Vicki slipped out of the room behind Mark, whispering a prayer. "Please, God, protect us."

A room at the end of the hall was open and

Mark ran for it. Vicki ducked inside and realized it was the second floor maid's station. Mark closed the door quietly and Vicki looked around. Cleaning supplies, sheets, blankets, and towels were stored neatly on shelves. In the corner, two carts, fully stocked.

"Maybe they have a laundry chute," Vicki said.

They searched but couldn't find one. "Must be someplace else in the building."

"What about a fire escape?" Vicki said. "A building this size has to have one."

Mark checked on the back of the door for directions in case of a fire. "It only shows stairs."

Vicki opened a locker and found a maid's dress. She held it up and looked at Mark. "You think you could fit on the bottom of one of those carts?"

Mark pulled away towels and supplies from the bottom and tried to squeeze onto it, but his legs stuck out.

"We'd better just make a run for it," Vicki said. "The longer we wait—"

Footsteps in the hall. Wheels squeaking. Vicki looked for a place to hide but it was too late. The door opened and a black woman backed in, pulling her cart. She hummed a familiar tune.

Before they could run, the woman turned

and was so startled that she fell back, a hand on her chest.

The woman had the mark of the true believer!

"Land sakes, you two just about scared me to death," she said with a thick Southern accent. She looked them over and smiled when she saw their marks. "So you're what all the commotion is about."

Mark started to explain, but the woman put her hand in the air as someone ran down the hall. "GC officers are checking each room," she whispered. "What did you two do?"

A radio squawked. "Check 264! Front desk says they have a key to that room."

Vicki trembled as she whispered, "We thought we were helping another believer but the GC tricked us."

"Mm mm mm," the black woman said. "Looks like it's time for me to take out the trash." She pointed to two huge garbage cans with rollers on the bottom.

Mark nodded and helped Vicki inside one. He climbed in the other, and the woman piled wet towels and trash on top of them. "Can you still breathe?" she said.

"We're fine," Mark whispered.

The woman hummed the tune again, stopping long enough to say, "My job's the same as the Lord's in a way. I take the trash out and make sure it gets put in the right place. He takes our trash and puts it on the cross where Jesus can take care of it. Simple as that. Hmm hmm hmm hmm . . ."

The woman wheeled the two trash cans down the corridor. Vicki heard the splash of the pool and the hum of the soda machine as they rolled along.

Someone yelled, "Florence! There are two teenagers running around here. If you see them, holler."

"All right, then," Florence said at the top of her lungs, "I will!"

The wheels squeaked as Florence pushed and pulled the trash cans. "I sure hope those kids haven't done anything to get the Global Community upset. That would be just awful."

Vicki smiled. Moments before she had felt there was no way out of the hotel. Now she felt cared for and safe.

A service elevator opened and Florence pushed them inside. "Look at that itty-bitty little camera up there in the corner, watching everything I do. I tell you, if I was trying to get away, I'd stay right where I was in case somebody's watching."

Vicki noticed a strong smell when they made it outside. She peeked over the edge and saw a huge, green garbage container at the edge of the building. Florence wheeled the two containers close, turned them on their sides, out of sight, and sighed. "Now I hope you two won't come round here very often, 'cause you nearly gave old Florence a heart attack."

"How will we ever repay you?" Vicki said, her voice muffled by the trash and wet towels.

"Honey, you can repay me by getting out of here in one piece and staying away from all these people who want to chop your head off. I'll go back inside while you two climb out of there and get over the fence. Directly I'll come back for my trash cans and hopefully nobody'll know the difference."

"Wait," Vicki said. "That song you were humming. What's it called?"

Florence laughed. "Everybody knows 'Amazing Grace, how sweet the sound.' Learned it from Momma when I was little. Wish I'd have listened to her when she tried to tell me about God, but I expect I'll be seeing her again one of these days." Florence hummed the old hymn as she walked back into the hotel.

Vicki and Mark crawled out, climbed to the top of the bin above, and hopped over the fence. They crouched low, walking between newly planted pine trees that shielded them from view of the building and the street. Two blocks away from the hotel, they cut across the street and made their way back to the car.

Vicki's heart pounded as they neared the parking lot. Mark held up a hand and told Vicki to wait in the alley. When they were sure no GC squad cars were nearby, Mark casually walked to the car, started it, and returned.

Mark drove away from the hotel, using side streets until they found their bearings and headed north. Vicki called the safe house in Wisconsin and Shelly answered.

"It was all a hoax, Shel. You should have seen Claudia's face when we came out of that room. She hated us."

"You tried," Shelly said. "And you're safe. That's what's important."

Vicki asked Shelly and the kids to pray that Anita and other gang members would believe the truth.

"We've been praying for you guys non-stop," Shelly said. "Charlie even prayed that God would send an angel to show you the way back."

Vicki smiled. "Tell Charlie God answered his prayer with a woman named Florence."

After she hung up, Vicki thought of Claudia. When the girl had first written, Vicki sensed something was wrong. Claudia's bosses had probably written her notes.

Vicki remembered the questions she had asked herself after the first e-mail. *How do I know the right thing to do when the choices aren't clear? How do I follow my heart when my heart doesn't know what to do?*

"Why do you think Claudia didn't have the mark of Carpathia?" Vicki said to Mark.

"They probably thought it would give her away if we had a face to face with her. That also explains why she didn't have sores."

Vicki sighed and vowed never again to dismiss her feelings about such things. As Mark drove north, Vicki quietly hummed and thought of Florence.

EIGHT

The Conversation

DARRION Stahley breathed a sigh of relief when she heard Vicki was okay. The kids focused their prayer effort on Manny, his sister, and the gang members.

In addition to her work on the kids' Web site, Darrion kept an eye on what was going on in Israel. She hadn't heard anything from Judd and Lionel and hoped they would call. Global Community Network News reported the strange sickness affecting people all over the world, but they didn't connect the sores with the mark of Carpathia.

One commentator speaking about the scene at the temple said the actions of the potentate showed his true leadership abilities. "You saw in the Holy of Holies the perfect use of force when it was needed. Anyone who disregards a direct order from this man deserves death."

A woman nodded in agreement. "But the skill and diplomacy of Potentate Carpathia is also evident. You saw his humility. Even though the temple is now his 'house,' as he called it, he stooped to negotiate with this Micah, the monklike character in the robe."

"And we receive word now that His Excellency the potentate guarantees healing from the affliction of sores by 2100 hours Carpathian Time."

Darrion tuned out the news and studied the kids' Web site. More people were writing than ever before, and Darrion felt privileged to attach information to each e-mail about how to become a believer. Some people wrote heart-wrenching notes asking how to get rid of the sores that had broken out all over their bodies. Darrion knew these people had taken the mark of Carpathia.

The phone rang and Darrion picked up.

It was Judd. "We're headed to Masada, but I have a situation here," he said. "I lost contact with Lionel. If you hear from him, tell him where I'm going and have him call me."

Darrion made sure she had the right phone number for Judd. "Anything else?"

"Yeah, I just got a call from Chang in New Babylon. They're having trouble reaching the guy who's setting up all the computer stuff in Petra, David Hassid."

"What could have happened?" Darrion said.

"Chang says Mr. Hassid was alone and there may have been some GC Peacekeepers left in the area. Have everyone pray he'll be okay and that the equipment won't fall into the wrong hands."

As Darrion wrote down the information, Judd asked about Vicki. Darrion told him what had happened in Des Plaines.

"When she gets back, have her call me too," Judd said.

※

Lionel noticed a line of helicopters to their left and assumed they were heading for Masada. In a short time, thousands of curious Israelis had converged on the fabled fortress.

Westin parked as close as he could, and everyone got out and began the long climb up the stone steps. As they walked, people talked about Carpathia's actions in the temple and what he might do next. Someone near Lionel questioned whether the whole crowd could be transported to Petra. Others walked in silence, seemingly drawn to the ancient site.

Lionel knew that God was calling these people to follow him, but would they be convinced?

Judd let Mr. Stein and the others walk ahead to Masada while he stayed in the car. Huge crowds moved on foot and helicopters landed nearby, filled with anxious participants. Judd was sure it would be after dark before Chaim would speak. He looked at his watch and counted the hours before Carpathia's attack.

Judd felt angry at Lionel for getting separated. He had made it clear many times that they had to stick together, and Lionel had wandered off with Sam. Judd lay down in the back of the rabbi's car and put an arm over his forehead.

Judd had no trouble thinking the worst about people. When a problem arose, he found someone to blame. *Maybe it's not Lionel's fault,* he thought. *Lionel wasn't trying to get separated. It just happened.*

Judd thought about the people he had hurt with his quick anger. He had been insensitive to Ryan Daley several times, and Judd regretted that he would never get to apologize and make things right.

As Judd listened to the noise outside, he smiled. Ryan would have loved to see God reaching more and more people around the world.

What about the others I've hurt? Judd thought. *Mark and Shelly . . . and Vicki.*

Judd cringed when he thought of what he had said about Vicki in his last conversation with Shelly. Vicki had been out late with some guy in Iowa, and Judd had assumed the worst. Judd shook his head and rubbed his eyes. He had to stop saying the first thing that came into his mind.

The phone startled Judd and he sat up, disoriented. He had no idea how long he had been there, but the sun was going down and people were still coming into Masada.

"Judd, it's Lionel. Where are you, man?"

"I'm in a car about a mile away from the fortress. How about you?"

"I'm inside with Sam and Mr. Stein. He told me about your ride with Rabbi Ben-Eliezar."

"Did you fly down in a chopper?" Judd said.

"Westin brought us," Lionel said, and he explained what had happened to them. "They're setting up a small medical tent outside the fortress. Why don't you meet me there in an hour?"

Judd agreed and sat back. He didn't want to frighten Lionel with the information about the impending attack, so he decided to tell him when they met at the tent.

Vicki slept while Mark drove toward Wisconsin. She awoke several times to find Mark pulled over on a side street or a crowded parking lot making sure they didn't cross paths with any GC vehicles.

While she was awake, Vicki found herself praying for Manny and wondering how the other gang members had reacted to his message. She thought about Anita and her difficult life. The girl wasn't a believer, but she had still resisted the mark of the beast.

Vicki dialed the safe house and Shelly answered. There was noise in the background, and Shelly said the hideout seemed crowded. "The Fogartys and Cheryl have been praying for you a lot."

"Tell them I appreciate it. We'll talk about the overcrowding issue when we get back."

"Colin already has a plan," Shelly said. "One of his friends has started an underground group in the western part of the state. Charlie's excited and wants to take Phoenix, and some of the others think it's a good idea."

"Okay, but don't decide anything until we get there."

"Oh, and Darrion said to tell you she talked with Judd."

"Where is he?"

"Still in Israel, at Masada. And get this, he

told Darrion to have you call him as soon as you get back."

"Did she say what he wanted to talk about?"

"Nope. You should call him."

※

Judd walked with a crowd of excited Israelis approaching Masada. Men spoke with disgust about Carpathia. "Yes, but I am equally distrustful of this Micah," one man said. "You know he will talk to us about Jesus being the Messiah."

"I'll listen to anyone if they can scare Carpathia away," the man said. "Did you see the way Micah spoke to Nicolae?"

Thousands milled around inside the fortress, while others stayed outside. Many carried a simple meal of bread and cheese and shared with those who had nothing. As Judd came close to the medical tent being set up, his phone rang.

"Judd, it's Vicki. I heard you wanted to talk."

Judd smiled. "Are you back in Wisconsin already?"

"Almost. Mark just fueled up and is getting something to eat. We're both pretty tired."

"Darrion told me about your brush with the GC. Sounded pretty hairy."

"You're saying that from Israel where

Carpathia could bomb you any minute. That's the hairiest place on earth right now."

Judd hesitated and the silence unnerved him. Vicki asked what Masada was like and he tried to describe it. "I wish you could be here. I have a feeling a lot of Israelis are going to believe once Micah—Dr. Rosenzweig—talks."

"Is that who Micah is?" Vicki said. "I didn't recognize his voice." She paused. "I was thinking how long you and Lionel have been over there. Do you realize when we last saw you two?"

"When you're in the middle of everything, time goes pretty fast. Then when I stop to think about it . . . well, it feels like decades since we've seen each other."

Vicki gave a nervous laugh. "So, are you headed home?"

"I can't say for sure, but I've been having these feelings like our time here is about over." Judd took a deep breath and turned from the crowd, finding a place behind the tent where no one could hear him. "Vicki, I know we've talked about this, and maybe now's not the time . . ."

"No, go ahead."

"We've had our problems, butting heads and lots of angry words. I want you to know

I'm really sorry for the stupid stuff I've done. I think maybe God brought me over here to knock some of the rough edges off. Lionel's been a big help with that."

Vicki chuckled. "He's been a good friend to both of us."

"I was thinking about Ryan earlier and how hard I was on him. You always stuck up for him."

"You mean about Phoenix?" Vicki said.

"I was on him a lot for different things. I wish I could take all that back."

"Ryan knew how much you cared. I'm sure of it. And while you're apologizing, I have to admit I haven't been the best friend. I was always thinking you were looking down on me because my family wasn't as rich as your family."

"You know that stuff doesn't mean anything now," Judd said. "When the disappearances happened, we were all in the same condition. We needed God. That was the only thing that mattered."

"Soooo," Vicki said. "What does this mean?"

Judd glanced at the front of the tent and saw Lionel. He waved and Lionel started over. "I think it means when I get back, we should take some time and talk."

"Good," Vicki said. "I hope you get back sooner rather than later."

Judd said good-bye and handed the phone to Lionel. He talked with Vicki a few moments and hung up. "So you two are back on speaking terms?"

Judd smiled and put an arm around Lionel. He told him what Chang had said about Carpathia's plans. "I've been thinking we ought to go home."

"You and me both," Lionel said. "Westin talked with Z-Van again a few minutes ago and tried to convince him to head back to the States before things blow up here."

"What did he say?"

"No luck. Z-Van's committed to a concert that'll be beamed by satellite all around the world. The GC is hoping it will encourage people in the less populated areas to come out and get their Nicolae tattoo."

Judd looked at the massive crowd now pushing its way up the steps of the fortress. "It'll take more than a couple songs from The Four Horsemen—"

Lionel held up a hand. "Is that who I think it is?"

Judd turned and saw two women helping a man with medical supplies. Judd recognized Mac McCullum, their friend from the Tribulation Force.

Judd and Lionel yelled and rushed to the edge of the tent.

Mac smiled and shook hands with the two. He was surprised but glad they were reaching out to unbelievers. "Sorry I'm not more excited right now. We just got some bad news."

"What's that?" Judd said.

"One of our members, David Hassid, was killed earlier today." Mac explained that David was alone at Petra setting up their computer equipment when two GC Peace-keepers stumbled upon him. "They didn't find the equipment, but needless to say, we're all pretty upset."

Judd's mind reeled. He had hoped the protection of God would cover all believers involved in the operation. If David Hassid was dead, that meant other believers might die.

Will God protect Lionel, Sam, and Mr. Stein? Judd thought. *Will he protect me?*

NINE

Micah's Message

JUDD and Lionel talked briefly with two women helping Mac, Hannah Palemoon and Leah Rose. Leah had come from the States to help in Operation Eagle, while Hannah had worked in New Babylon. Leah gave Judd and Lionel food, and they thanked her.

Lionel led Judd up the crowded stairway to rejoin Mr. Stein and Sam. As they slowly inched through the masses, Judd asked Lionel how they should get home.

"Westin's a man of his word. He told us he'd take us back. If anybody can get us there, he can."

Judd's phone rang and it was Chang. While Judd talked, Lionel went ahead, taking some food to his friends who were seated on a ledge above them. The phone beeped a low-battery message, so Judd quickly told

Chang what was happening at Masada. Chang informed him that Dr. Rosenzweig was there waiting for the chance to speak.

"There are no speakers or microphones," Judd said. "How are all these people going to hear him?"

"There wasn't time to set any of that up," Chang said. "I'm praying God will enable everyone to hear."

"Any problems with the airlift out of Jerusalem?"

"The return runs from Petra to the Mount of Olives have been delayed slightly, but things have gone smoothly. It seems a miracle that such a massive relocation has not had one mechanical failure." Chang paused. "I didn't expect one thing—my mother e-mailed a message."

Judd had met Mrs. Wong in New Babylon and knew she wasn't a believer. "Has she taken the mark of Carpathia?"

"I don't think so. She said my father was upset about what Carpathia did in Jerusalem and he wondered what I would think about it."

"Good," Judd said. "They both sound more open to the truth."

"Perhaps. My mother is the one who has visited Tsion Ben-Judah's Web site. She wanted to know how he could predict things so accurately."

"I'll tell the others here and we'll pray for them," Judd said. "Did you write back?"

"Yes. I pleaded with her to give her life to God before it is too late."

"I hope one day she'll be part of the Tribulation Force," Judd said.

Chang's voice broke up and the phone finally went dead. Judd ran to the Hummer and plugged in the recharger, then found Mr. Stein and the others. The sun had gone down and Judd closed his eyes and listened to the noise of thousands of Israelis talking among themselves. Judd checked his watch. It was only an hour before the lifting of the plague.

Will God allow Carpathia to bomb these people? Judd thought.

Mr. Stein motioned to a robed figure at the other end of the fortress. The man's head was bowed in prayer. Mr. Stein joined hands with Judd and the others. "Righteous Father, those gathered here have not known you, but we ask that you will open ears and eyes tonight, and give your servant a strong voice and mind. We ask in the name of Jesus, amen."

As Mr. Stein finished, Dr. Rosenzweig stood on high ground and raised his arms.

People around the fortress pointed, and Judd noticed that those outside became quiet.

"My friends," Micah said with power, "I cannot guarantee your safety here tonight. Your very presence makes you an enemy and a threat to the ruler of this world, and when the plague of sores upon his people is lifted at nine o'clock tonight, they may target you with a vengeance."

Judd watched the man's lips move. It looked like a foreign movie dubbed into English. Mr. Stein leaned over and whispered, "He is speaking in Hebrew, but we understand in English."

"I will keep my remarks brief," Dr. Rosenzweig said, "but I will be asking you to make a decision that will change your destiny. If you agree with me and make this commitment, cars, trucks, and helicopters will ferry you to a place of refuge. If you do not, you may return to your homes and face the gruesome choice between the guillotine or the mark of loyalty to the man who sat in your temple this very day and proclaimed himself god. He is the man who defiled God's house with murder and with the blood of swine, who installed his own throne and the very image of himself in the Holy of Holies, who put an end to all sacrifices to the true and living God, and who withdrew his promise of peace for Israel."

Judd looked at the people around him. No one strained or acted like they couldn't hear.

"I must tell you sadly that many of you will make that choice. You will choose sin over God. You will choose pride and selfishness and life over the threat of death. Some of you have already rejected God's gift so many times that your heart has been hardened. And though your risky sojourn to this meeting may indicate a change of mind on your part, it is too late for a change of heart. Only God knows.

"Because of who you are and where you come from, and because of who I am and where I come from, we can stipulate that we agree on many things. We believe there is one God, creator of the universe and sustainer of life, that all good and perfect things come from him alone. But I tell you that the disappearances that ravaged our world three and a half years ago were the work of his Son, the Messiah, who was foretold in the Scriptures and whose prophecies did Jesus of Nazareth, the Christ, fulfill."

※

Vicki was mobbed as she walked into Colin Dial's home. Mark gave the full story of

Manny's decision to stay with the gang and the kids prayed for him, his sister, and that Hector would respond to the truth.

Darrion burst through the door, hugged Vicki, and urged the kids to follow her downstairs to hear the meeting at Masada.

"How are you getting it?" Mark said.

"Chang found a way to send it," Darrion said.

Mark guessed by the tinny sound that they were using a cell phone. However they were doing it, Dr. Rosenzweig's voice was clear.

The room was electrified as he spoke of Jesus as the Messiah the Jews had long awaited. He gave prophecy after prophecy from the Scriptures that Jesus had fulfilled. Vicki noticed Tom and Josey Fogarty furiously taking notes.

"He is the only One who could be the Messiah," Dr. Rosenzweig declared. "He also died unlike anyone else in history. He gave himself willingly as a sacrifice and then proved himself worthy when God raised him from the dead. Even skeptics and unbelievers have called Jesus the most influential person in history.

"Of the billions and billions of people who have ever lived, One stands head and shoulders above the rest in terms of influence. More schools, colleges, hospitals, and orphanages have been started because of him than because of anyone else. More art was created, more music written, and more humanitarian acts performed due to him and his influence than anyone else ever. Great international encyclopedias devote twenty thousand words to describing him and his influence on the world. Even our calendar is based on his birth. And all this he accomplished in a public ministry that lasted just three and a half years!

"Jesus of Nazareth, Son of God, Savior of the world, and Messiah, predicted that he would build his church and the gates of hell would not prevail against it. Centuries after his public, unmerciful mocking, his persecution and martyrdom, billions claimed membership in his church, making it by far the largest religion in the world. And when he returned, as he said he would, to take his faithful to heaven, the disappearance of so many had the most profound impact on this globe that man has ever seen.

"Messiah was to be born in Bethlehem to a virgin, to live a sinless life, to serve as God's spotless Lamb of sacrifice, to give himself willingly to die on a cross for the sins of the world, to rise again three days later, and to sit at the right hand of God the Father Almighty.

Jesus fulfilled these and all the other 109 prophecies, proving he is the Son of God."

Vicki closed her eyes and tried to picture the gathering in Masada. She wondered if, at that same moment, Manny might be speaking to the gang, using different words, but giving the same message.

"Tonight, Messiah calls to you from down through the ages. He is the answer to your condition. He offers forgiveness for your sins. He paid the penalty for you. As the most prolific writer of Scripture, a Jew himself, wrote, 'If you confess with your mouth the Lord Jesus and believe in your heart that God has raised him from the dead, you will be saved. For with the heart one believes unto righteousness, and with the mouth confession is made unto salvation. For the Scripture says, "Whoever believes on him will not be put to shame." For there is no distinction between Jew and Greek, for the same Lord over all is rich to all who call upon him. For whoever calls on the name of the Lord shall be saved.'

"For years skeptics have made fun of the evangelist's plea, 'Do you want to be saved tonight?' and yet that is what I ask you right now. Do not expect God to be fooled. Be not deceived. God will not be mocked. Do not do this to avoid a confrontation with

Antichrist. You need to be saved because you cannot save yourself.

"The cost is great but the reward greater. This may cost you your freedom, your family, your very head. You may not survive the journey to safety. But you will spend eternity with God, worshiping the Lord Christ, Messiah, Jesus."

The kids didn't make a sound. Vicki prayed silently for the people in Masada and that Judd and Lionel would soon return.

Judd stood, his mouth open, excited at what was happening around him. Seeing Chaim Rosenzweig speak with such authority to so many Israelis was worth any danger he would face. Judd knew the Bible predicted that Jewish people would one day recognize Jesus as Messiah. Could this be the day?

As Chaim listed more prophecies Jesus fulfilled, Judd noticed people standing, responding to the message. People hung on every word. As Dr. Rosenzweig came to the end of his presentation, he invited people to pray with him. All around the fortress, inside and out, Israelis repeated the prayer. Judd looked over the crowd and saw many with the mark of God on their foreheads. Dr.

Rosenzweig walked down the steps and thousands followed him.

Judd drew close as Mr. Stein talked with Rabbi Ben-Eliezar and his wife.

"Jesus is the fulfillment of all of those prophecies," Mr. Stein said.

The rabbi put a hand through his hair. "To say that Jesus is the Jewish Messiah is to go against everything I have been taught. I don't know . . ."

Mr. Stein lowered his voice. "Which is better? To continue believing a teaching that is in error or to believe the truth?"

Mr. Stein turned to Mrs. Ben-Eliezar. "You have heard the evidence. You know Nicolae Carpathia is anti-God. God has spared your lives for this time. But you must make your decision."

The woman huddled close to her husband. "I don't think we have a choice, Ethan. To put our trust in Jesus seems like spiritual suicide, but I feel in my heart that we may have been wrong all these years."

The rabbi gave Mr. Stein a terrified look. His eyes flashed as he turned to his wife. "How could I have been so blind? I have trampled the gift of God all of these years."

"Give your lives to the master now," Mr. Stein said. "Don't wait another minute."

"I can't remember the prayer," the rabbi said. "Will you help us?"

Mr. Stein nodded and the rabbi and his wife repeated his words. "Dear God, I know that I am separated from you because I am a sinner. I believe Jesus is the Messiah and that he died on the cross to pay the penalty for my sins. I believe he rose again the third day and that by receiving his gift of love I will have the power to become a son of God because I believe on his name. Thank you for hearing me and saving me, and I pledge the rest of my life to you."

Rabbi Ben-Eliezar and his wife looked up, and Judd saw the mark of the believer on their foreheads. Mr. Stein wept with them and Judd turned away. What he saw both thrilled and horrified him. Dr. Rosenzweig moved toward hundreds of vehicles and helicopters that waited in long lines. But thousands of others ran from Masada. They looked hopeless, like people with no direction, fear etched on their faces. They called out, looking for rides back to Jerusalem.

Judd shuddered when he thought of all those people turning their backs on God. Judd had done the same thing many times when he was younger.

Is this their last chance? he thought.

TEN

Nicolae's Plan

LIONEL and Sam helped Mac and the others tear down the medical tent and load it in a truck. People streamed out of Masada and into helicopters, cars, and trucks.

When the supplies were loaded, Mac yelled for new believers to get in the back of the truck. "Next stop, Petra!"

Israelis streamed toward them. One grabbed Sam by the arm. "When we pray to God now, should we pray to Jesus?" he said.

As Sam talked with him, Leah, a member of the Tribulation Force, turned to Lionel. "Are you coming with us?"

Lionel looked around for Judd. He didn't want to leave again without talking with his friend. Before Lionel could answer, Sam said, "I'll go."

"Then get in," Leah said. "And you?"

"I have to talk to my friend," Lionel said. "Go ahead."

Leah ran to the front and hopped in. Sam shook hands with Lionel and smiled. "Thanks for everything you've done. I hope to see you at Petra."

"If not," Lionel said, "call or write us. I want to hear about everything."

Sam jumped in the back of the truck. As they drove away, the Israelis peppered Sam with questions.

※

Judd and Mr. Stein joined Lionel at the loading area. Westin honked the Humvee's horn and waved.

"Somebody should go with these people back to Jerusalem," Lionel said. "Maybe they can be convinced of the truth."

Mr. Stein frowned. "I'm afraid they have hardened their hearts. If what they heard from Micah did not persuade them, I fear they are destined to choose Carpathia over God."

Judd studied the scores of choppers and vehicles recruited from around the world. The amount of work to get all these people together was staggering.

Lionel looked at Judd. "What do we do?"

Before Judd could answer, GC vehicles

rumbled up with loudspeakers mounted on top. "The entire state of Israel has been declared a no-fly zone by the Global Community Security and Intelligence director. All civilian aircraft, take fair warning: Any non-GC craft determined to be over Israeli airspace runs the risk of destruction.

"The potentate himself has also decreed martial law and has instituted a curfew on civilian vehicular traffic in Israel. Violators are subject to arrest.

"Due to the severity of the affliction that has befallen GC personnel, these curfews are required. Only a skeleton crew of workers is available to maintain order.

"His Excellency reminds citizens that he has effected a relief from the plague as of 2100 hours, and the populace should plan to celebrate with him at daybreak."

Judd looked at his watch. It was a few minutes before nine. If these announcements were correct, new believers loading into the helicopters were flying to their deaths.

Mr. Stein started toward a quickly filling chopper. "Are you coming?"

Westin honked again. "I've got two more spots, guys, come on!"

Judd hesitated, knowing the decision he was about to make might change the course of their lives forever. In the dust and noise of motors and GC announcements, Judd grabbed Lionel by the shoulder and pulled him toward the Hummer.

Over the din of the helicopters, Judd heard Mr. Stein yell, "He is risen!"

"He is risen indeed!" Judd and Lionel yelled back.

***

While Mark got some needed sleep, Vicki pulled Shelly aside and told her about her conversation with Judd.

Shelly put a hand over her mouth. "How do you feel about it?" she said.

"Excited. A little scared. I've liked Judd as a friend for a long time. It feels like something's changed with him."

"Did he talk about the girl he was involved with?"

"Nada?" Vicki said. "No, he didn't mention her. But I'm sure he'll tell me all about it when he gets back."

Shelly ran her tongue over her lower lip and tilted her head back. "Since we're being honest about guys, I have a confession."

Vicki grinned, anticipating what was coming.

"Conrad and I have become pretty good friends since our trip out west. We've been doing a Bible study together. And he writes me letters. Isn't it romantic?"

"If anything can be romantic these days, it's writing letters to somebody staying in the same house with you. Does anybody know?"

"We've kept it pretty quiet, but I think Charlie does."

Vicki smiled. "I have to remember that when Judd comes back."

Conrad knocked on the door and peeked in. Shelly winked at him. "I just told Vicki."

"I'm happy for you two," Vicki said.

Conrad nodded. "Vicki, there's something on the news I think you'll want to see."

Darrion turned the sound up as Vicki came into the main meeting room. ". . . found in an alley behind this building. Some experts believe there is a possible border war brewing among the gangs. But Global Community Peacekeepers don't think that's the case. They say the death of this man is payback for information he gave authorities after his arrest a few weeks ago."

Manny Aguilara's photo flashed on the screen. "Global Community Peacekeepers

have revealed that this man escaped from
a Global Community jail, aided by gang
members. This happened after he gave information incriminating gang leader Hector
Rodriguez. Aguilara's death—"

Vicki put a hand over her mouth, waved,
and asked them to turn the TV off. When she
could talk, she said, "Manny would be alive
if he had come back with us."

Conrad put a hand on her shoulder. "He
sent an e-mail for you. We just found it."

Vicki took the printed page, wiped her
eyes, and read.

> Vicki, Mark, and the rest of the Young
> Tribulation Force,
>
> I want to thank you for being so kind
> and helping me. You forgave me for not
> telling you the truth, but I believe it has
> turned out for the best.
>
> They've called a meeting and I'm to
> speak in front of a large group of gang
> members in a few minutes. I'm praying that
> God will open their eyes. I've been talking
> to my sister about God, and she listens but
> has not yet prayed. I wish one of you could
> be here or Zeke Sr. You would know exactly
> what to say.
>
> I will write and tell you what happened
> afterward. I hope you were able to find

Claudia and get her to safety. Please remember to pray for me, as I will be praying for you.

Sincerely,
Manny

Vicki stared at the letter and wondered what had happened in that meeting. Had the group planned to kill Manny all along? Had he even been able to tell them about God? Vicki closed her eyes and pictured Zeke welcoming Manny in heaven. She would see them again. The only question was, how soon?

⁕

Judd waited outside the Humvee as long as he could, admiring the line of helicopters and vehicles headed for Petra. Westin shouted for him to get in when everyone was ready, and Judd made sure he had a seat by the window. Several Israelis who had not prayed with Dr. Rosenzweig jammed into the vehicle, acting fidgety about the three believers on board.

"You don't have to worry about us," Westin said. "We'll get you back to Jerusalem in one piece. What you do from there is your business."

The sky filled with Operation Eagle choppers. Soon, what Judd assumed was a squadron of GC choppers approached. A few GC airplanes also flew cautiously above the line of Operation Eagle aircraft.

Lionel nudged Judd. "What are we going to do in Jerusalem?"

"See if we can get back home before another war breaks out," Judd said.

"Do you really think there will be war?" a young man beside Lionel said.

Westin looked in the rearview mirror. "Knowing how much Carpathia hates followers of Jesus *and* Jewish people, and seeing as how the Bible predicts another great war, I don't think there's any way to deny it."

Judd glanced at his watch. It was now well past the 9 P.M. deadline, and as Judd had feared, GC Peacekeepers and Morale Monitors seemed on a mission to head off the fleeing Israelis. Westin flipped on the video scanner, and Judd couldn't believe how many cars, buses, and trucks were on the road. GC squad cars passed them with lights flashing.

"Can you hear any GC transmissions?" Judd asked Westin.

Westin tuned in a GC frequency. Officers gave commands and coded communication Judd couldn't understand.

"I know what they're saying," an Israeli who

had worked for the GC said. "They're telling them to block the traffic heading toward Petra first. The initial squad cars are supposed to stop them. The second wave, up ahead, is supposed to stop us and search our vehicles."

For ten minutes GC squad cars passed. There were so many that Judd lost count and wondered how many aircraft the GC had sent.

"I thought they were supposed to celebrate getting over their sores," Lionel said.

Westin leaned forward in his seat and peered out the windshield. "I think they *are* celebrating."

"But Micah was clear," Lionel said. "They're not supposed to hurt any of God's chosen people or there's going to be a worse plague."

"Does that mean us too?" one of the men in the back said.

"If you want God's protection," Westin said, "ask Jesus to forgive you—"

"Never!" the man shouted.

"Then I can't promise you won't suffer the same fate," Westin said.

The Israelis talked among themselves about the locusts, the fiery hail, the water turned to blood, and other plagues they had experienced in the past few years. Judd wanted to shake them, repeat Chaim's message, anything.

A line of bright lights spread out on the road ahead of them and Westin slowed. "I don't like the looks of this." He rolled down his window and Judd heard loudspeakers.

"By order of Potentate Carpathia, each vehicle must stop immediately. You are violating a curfew established by the potentate himself."

A few vehicles in front slowed and came to a stop. Westin gunned the engine and pulled off the road, kicking up dust behind them.

Again the GC speakers came alive. "By authority of the Global Community and its risen potentate and lord, His Excellency Nicolae Carpathia, you are commanded to stop at once and surrender. Your passengers and cargo will be impounded by the Global Community. If you are in compliance with the loyalty mark, you will be free to go."

"Which means we're dead if we stop," Judd said.

"You got it," Westin said. "They take us in and they'll make us take Carpathia's mark or face the blade."

"I don't get what's so wrong with an identifying mark," an Israeli said.

"After what that monster did in the temple today?" another said. "I'll never comply."

"Anybody who wants to get out and follow the GC, do it right now," Westin said. He

slammed on his brakes and slid into a huge
culvert Judd assumed had been made during
the wrath of the Lamb earthquake.

Westin unlocked the doors but no one
moved. "All right then, fasten your seat belts.
It might get a little bumpy."

Judd's mind raced, trying to remember all
Tsion Ben-Judah had said. Judd believed
Petra would have God's protection, but what
about believers headed for Jerusalem with a
vehicle filled with unbelievers? Judd closed
his eyes and breathed a brief prayer as Westin
put the Hummer into four-wheel drive and
barreled out of the crater. The vehicle seemed
to go straight up, then straight back down a
rocky hillside.

Judd remembered going on a ride at a mall
when he was younger. The video display and
the motion of the car made it feel like he was
actually hurtling through space. Now he was
experiencing a thrill ride of another kind on
the ground in Israel.

Judd leaned forward to watch the 3-D
viewer in front. A line of choppers stretched
miles behind them. He focused on one
aircraft that seemed to hover above the
others, and a smaller chopper pulled in
beside it. The smaller helicopter appeared to

be a Global Community craft and Judd wondered if it was armed.

Westin careened over curbs and torn-up streets. They passed the line of GC squad cars along with other vehicles following Westin's lead. Behind them, half the GC force was in hot pursuit.

Judd glanced at the grid again. Choppers remained in line except for the two choppers hovering above. The smaller one quickly moved back, like an angry bull ready to charge. The larger chopper held its position until something flashed onscreen. *Bullets!*

The smaller craft fired at close range. Judd closed his eyes and waited for the explosion.

ELEVEN

Over the Edge

JUDD looked again in horror as bursts of gunfire appeared on the screen in front of him. Judd had seen movies where these types of guns blew planes and helicopters out of the sky.

The bullets entered the rear of the bigger chopper, flashed inside the cabin, and exited the front, but there was no explosion, no ball of flame, no helicopter falling from the sky like Judd expected. Instead, the Operation Eagle bird hovered as if nothing had happened.

A Global Community chopper in front of the Operation Eagle bird veered crazily, its tail rotors struck by the bullets. It fell end over end and finally spun into the ground. A plume of smoke mushroomed from the wreckage.

"What was that?" Westin said.

Judd told him what he had seen and Lionel sat forward. "Maybe this is part of the protection God promised."

"Will we have that same protection?" an Israeli said.

"It's a trick," the man next to him said. "They're trying to scare us into believing."

"How could bullets go through metal and have no effect?" Westin said.

"The boy's making it up," another Israeli said. "I saw the screen and I don't think the bullets went through the first chopper. It was an accident."

Accident? Judd couldn't believe it. God had clearly done another miracle in front of their eyes and these people weren't seeing.

Westin continued around slower vehicles, avoiding traffic jams by jumping curbs, shooting around barricades, and spinning through loose rocks by the roadside. When they crested a hill, lights of vehicles headed toward Petra shone in the darkness. Judd wondered if they had made a mistake going back to Jerusalem. Could they remain safe that close to Carpathia?

Sam Goldberg held tight to a railing in the back of the vehicle driven by Mac McCullum.

The truck bounced and weaved on and off the road as they tried to outrun GC vehicles. Sam answered questions from the new believers around him. Some seemed angry that they had not listened earlier, while others simply wanted to know more.

"When did you become a believer?" one asked.

"How long until Messiah comes back?" another said.

"Will Carpathia attack Petra?" a woman behind Sam said.

Sam answered the questions as best he could as they rumbled south. "How many of you have read Rabbi Tsion Ben-Judah's Web site?" A few raised hands. "When we get to our destination, we'll see that you have teaching that will answer all your questions."

Sam glanced out the window as Operation Eagle vehicles evaded more GC Peacekeepers and Morale Monitors. Sam didn't understand why they hadn't been fired upon. How was God protecting them?

Leah Rose climbed into the front seat to talk with Mac, while the other American, Hannah Palemoon, remained quiet. Sam turned and was blinded by flashing lights behind him. GC Peacekeepers called through their PA system to pull over, but Mac kept going.

The car sped forward and Sam looked at Mac. He was still talking, not paying attention to the GC vehicle. Sam glanced over and saw a guard pointing a submachine gun at Mac.

Sam ducked, waiting for the gun's bullets to rip through the vehicle. Mac had picked up a cell phone and was talking with someone, but Sam couldn't make out the conversation.

"Are we going to be killed?" an Israeli next to Sam said.

Sam clenched his teeth. "I don't know."

Mac stopped in the middle of the road and the GC squad car pulled in front of them. When a Peacekeeper got out, Mac quickly reversed and shot past them and the chase began again. When the squad car pulled alongside, Mack slammed on the brakes and Sam shot forward.

"Sorry, friends!" Mac yelled. "Shoulda told y'all to buckle up!"

※

Judd phoned Chang in New Babylon again and the boy seemed harried, audio blaring in the background. Judd learned of Tsion's broadcast and had Westin turn on his radio. Sure enough, GCNN radio was airing Tsion, though they were trying to talk over him.

"Are you putting Tsion on the air?" Judd asked Chang.

"Who else?" Chang said.

"Any idea how Carpathia is reacting?"

"He's not happy. He executed Walter Moon for not getting Tsion off the air."

"He killed the supreme commander? How do you know?"

"We have a bug on his airplane, remember? And he's ranting like mad, ordering troops in Israel to shoot to kill. He wants every civilian plane destroyed." Chang paused, turning up Tsion's audio. Carpathia's voice rose in the background. "Listen to him," Chang said.

". . . Run them down. Crash their vehicles. Blow their heads off. As for Petra, wait until we know for certain Micah is there, then level it. Do we have what we need to do that?"

"We do, sir," someone said.

"In the meantime, someone, anyone, get— Ben-Judah—off—the—air!"

"I will pray him off, Your Worship," Leon Fortunato said.

"I will kill you if you do not shut up," Carpathia said.

"Quieting now, Highness," Leon said. Then, a gasp.

"What!?" Carpathia said.

"The water!" Fortunato said. "The ice!"

"What's happening?" Judd said, but Chang had put down the phone. Judd heard a faucet running.

Chang returned, out of breath. "Judd, the water has turned to blood!"

※

Vicki sent a reply to Manny's e-mail, hoping somehow Manny's sister would see it. As she surfed for any new information about what was going on in Israel, she noticed someone familiar on the television monitor and called the others together.

"Is that Dr. Ben-Judah?" Shelly said.

"Turn it up!" Conrad said.

Tsion sat in front of a mostly empty wall. "Greetings. It is a privilege for me to address the world through the miracle of technology. But as I am an unwelcome guest here, forgive me for being brief, and please lend me your attention."

Conrad switched channels, but Tsion was on every one of them. "I don't know how the Trib Force did this, but I'll bet Carpathia will go nuts when he sees it."

"I want to give my encouragement to all believers in Messiah," Tsion continued. "What we have witnessed at the temple should leave no doubt as to the identity of the man who calls himself potentate. His actions prove what we have been saying all along is true. Jesus Christ is the Messiah the Jews have long awaited, and he is coming back in power and majesty to rule and reign. Nicolae Carpathia is the Antichrist.

"As new believers gather in a place of safety, I would remind you that time is running out. If you have not yet taken the mark of Nicolae Carpathia, avoid it at all cost. God has seen fit to warn us and get our attention by sending plagues among us. They are his divine way of getting our attention. More are coming as God judges the evil one and his followers."

Dr. Ben-Judah spoke of the events of the past few days and commented on Carpathia's unbridled evil. In the past, Tsion had spoken much longer, and Vicki was surprised when he wrapped up his broadcast after only a few minutes.

"I close with a word to those who are right now traveling to Petra. I wish you Godspeed in your journey, and I promise to travel to meet you there personally and address the one million brothers and sisters in the Messiah."

"I wonder if they'll show *that* on television," Shelly said.

Sam had never felt so energized and terrified at the same time. He was busy helping believers understand their newfound faith, while their vehicle was pursued by GC Peacekeepers.

A GC squad car flew past them again and stopped within inches of Mac's bumper. Two men bounded from the car, yelling and waving their weapons. Mac drove past them again, and Sam watched the two level their weapons, then jump back into their vehicle. As they accelerated, Mac swerved left and braked, the rear of their vehicle sliding on the sand. Before the Peacekeepers knew what was happening, Mac had pulled in behind them.

"All right, we're going to try and . . ." Mac's voice trailed off as the taillights ahead flashed bright red. He slammed on his brakes and the truck slid a few feet.

Sam peered through the dust, wondering when the shooting would begin, but the squad car was nowhere in sight. It had somehow disappeared.

Operation Eagle cars and trucks roared in the distance, and behind them another line of GC cars approached. Suddenly, one of the new believers screamed, "The earth has opened up!"

Sam gasped at the chasm that had formed

behind them and to the right, and before the pursuing GC officers could stop, they plunged in. The screech of its siren grew faint as the car dropped out of sight.

Mac had jumped out and was now back in the vehicle, his voice quavery. "Our front tires are right on the edge. The thing must be hundreds of feet deep." Mac carefully backed up, using the four-wheel drive, and slowly tried to find a way around the opening.

"Here comes another one!" someone yelled behind Sam.

A GC car raced up to the edge and braked. Before the car slid into the crevasse, two Peacekeepers leaped out and rolled on the ground, their guns clattering. Everyone in the vehicle waited breathlessly as the two rose, found their rifles, and took aim at the truck.

"Duck!" Mac shouted.

Sam and the others dove for the floor of the truck, bumping heads and landing on one another. The guns cracked and Sam put his hands over his ears, not knowing what else to do. But the firing quickly stopped.

Sam peeked out the window as Mac opened his door. The Peacekeepers lay lifeless on the ground, their guns at their sides. Everyone got out and inspected the truck. Miraculously, there wasn't a scratch.

Mac's phone rang and Sam walked a few yards away to look into the chasm. He stood at the edge of what looked like the Grand Canyon.

"Better not get too close," Leah said. "Come on, let's get out of here."

Before they got back in the car, Mac told them he had just talked with the leader of Operation Eagle, Rayford Steele. "Dr. Ben-Judah is on the air right now, no doubt telling people the truth." He pointed into the air over Jerusalem. "And back there a war's going on."

Something in the distance burst into flames and fell to the earth in a fiery heap.

"War?" Sam said. "They're shooting down Operation Eagle helicopters?"

Mac smiled. "They're trying, but Rayford says they're only hitting each other."

※

Judd yelled as GC helicopters pursued a dozen Operation Eagle choppers above them. "They must not know they're protected! They're heading to Israel."

A GC chopper was hit and fell from the sky. Westin swerved and nearly hit a boulder as the ball of fire crashed twenty yards away. Debris from the impact scattered over the area and bounced off the roof of the Hummer.

The sky lit up with gunfire from GC attack choppers. It was an all-out war, but God was protecting his people.

Judd was excited when the radio feed had switched to Chaim Rosenzweig's message recorded at the Temple Mount. He hoped some of the Israelis in the car would reconsider their position about Jesus, but all he heard from them were groans and complaints to turn the radio down. Westin, of course, left it blaring.

Judd didn't want to bother Chang again, but he was so curious about Carpathia and Operation Eagle that he dialed him.

"We've got a problem here," Chang said. "Someone told Carpathia that Dr. Ben-Judah is coming to Petra. They're going to destroy Petra when he arrives."

"But Petra is safe, right?"

"I hope. And the blood problem is international. Be listening for reports. It's affecting the seas this time." Chang grew quiet. "I need you to pray."

"What for?" Judd said.

"They know someone's been listening to them from inside the Global Community. They're going to give lie detector tests here. And they say they'll kill the person who's guilty."

TWELVE

Going Home

JUDD wanted to talk with the Israelis in the Hummer one more time, but as Westin pulled into Jerusalem, the men jumped out and ran for their homes. They had listened to Dr. Rosenzweig's entire presentation and prayer over GCNN radio and still didn't respond.

Judd was terrified as hunks of molten steel, burning out of control, fell on roadways, buildings, and open fields. It looked like half the GC forces had been lost.

Chang called back and explained that he was safe from the GC for a while. "I hacked into the personnel files and created a record of my hospital stay for the last two days. They won't suspect a mole who's been recovering from boils."

"What about your computer?" Judd said. "If they search that—"

"It's fried. I saved everything, then crashed my hard drive. The laptop is stashed in my closet, so even if the GC find it, they won't be able to trace the broadcast or any of my activity. I'll be at my desk in the morning, ready for work."

✺

Vicki and the others watched the Israel coverage from the safety of Colin's home in Wisconsin. Live shots showed the falling GC aircraft. The GC was mistakenly killing its own by shooting at Operation Eagle.

GC forces on the ground fared no better, with reports that many vehicles had simply vanished. When it was learned that great holes had opened in the earth, rescue efforts were abandoned.

Vicki thought of Judd and hoped he would go with Lionel to Petra. From there, he might be able to find a flight home with a Tribulation Force volunteer.

Though the Global Community tried to downplay them, reports from around the world flooded in about the seas turning to blood. Beautiful vacation resorts became death sites as whales, fish, sharks, and every imaginable sea creature perished and rose to the surface. Ships radioed Mayday signals, saying they had run out of drinking water and were unable to get back to land.

Nicolae Carapthia spoke to the world from a secret studio in Israel, claiming that his Security and Intelligence personnel had identified Micah and his companion. As Carpathia spoke, Leon Fortunato stood in the background in his silly outfit, his lips moving in an unholy prayer.

"This Micah claimed to represent the rebels, but we now know he is an impostor who has used his trickery to create the great seawater catastrophe," Carpathia said. "Do not be dismayed. The enemies of the Global Community will be brought to justice, and just as the difficulty we have faced with the sores has passed, so this problem with the earth's waters will be overcome."

Aerial shots of the plague were unbelievable. Thick, gooey blood washed up on shores around the world. Fishing vessels were stuck, as if they were trying to sail through red syrup.

Vicki went to the computer to search for any word about Claudia Zander. With the help of Jim Dekker, who knew some of the GC passwords, Vicki was able to find a personnel report saying Claudia had been reassigned to another Morale Monitor division outside the Midwest. No further information was available.

"With the way the GC operates, she's lucky to be alive," Dekker said.

An alarm sounded inside the hideout. Colin had installed a motion sensor with video capabilities around the perimeter of his property. It usually went off around dusk with the movement of deer and other animals searching for food. Colin pulled up a camera shot and hit the reset button. "It's nothing, I'm sure."

❋

Sam was exhausted and running on adrenaline when Mac McCullum finally stopped their vehicle. Sam had talked with the new believers around him until his throat felt sore. The desert dust hadn't done much to help, but Sam thrilled at the taste of clean, clear water while the rest of the world was getting blood when they turned on a tap.

Sam had finally dozed after the GC chase ended and Mac had settled into the long drive through the desert. Mac relayed reports from Operation Eagle over his cell phone. Sam was excited to be part of the massive transport of a million Israelis to Petra, and he was eager to talk with Mr. Stein. The man had become like a father to him.

Hannah Palemoon had been quiet throughout the trip. She turned to Sam while most of the others were sleeping and asked if he was traveling alone.

Sam briefly told his story and how his father had been killed during the plague of horsemen. Hannah listened and wiped away a tear when Sam talked about his grief.

"Did you lose someone close to you?" Sam said.

Hannah nodded. "While I was in New Babylon, I met David Hassid, the one who organized this whole operation. He was killed by GC troops yesterday."

Sam put a hand on her shoulder. "Can I pray for you?"

Hannah nodded, too overcome to speak.

"Gracious Father, we thank you that we can come to you with our hurts. Thank you for the safety you provided tonight, and I pray for my new friend, that you would comfort her with your peace through this great sorrow over losing her good friend David. Encourage her in the days ahead, for we know it won't be long before Jesus returns in his majesty, and we will again see our friends who have died."

When Sam finished, Hannah wiped away tears and whispered, "Thank you."

∗

Judd and Lionel waited in the lobby of a posh hotel while Westin parked the Humvee in an underground lot. Though it was late, people milled about watching video coverage from the Global Community News Network. Hotel workers scrambled to supply their guests with soft drinks and juice. All of their bottled water was bloodred.

Westin returned and grabbed a key from the front desk. The three took an elevator to the fifth floor and found an envelope taped to the door. Westin opened it as they walked inside, shook his head, and handed the note to Judd.

> *Wes,*
>
> *Call me as soon as you get in. We're performing for His Excellency at the celebration of the lifting of the sickness tomorrow morning. Have the plane ready in case we need it afterward.*
>
> *Z.*

"You going to call him?" Lionel said.

"I have a better idea," Westin said. "Let's get a few hours' sleep, and then we'll fly out of here before sunup and get you two back to the States."

"Are you serious?" Judd said.

Westin smiled. "I'll drop you guys, then bring the plane back here and clear things up. He promised to get you back home, and I'm going to see it happens."

Sam was overcome with emotion when he saw the growing multitudes at Petra. It looked like the Israelites fleeing Egypt during the Exodus. Except this time they would not need to part the Red Sea to get to safety— they would enter through a narrow passage called a Siq.

Sam thanked Mac and the others for risking their lives.

Mac smiled and patted Sam's shoulder. "You need a ride anywhere, I'm there."

In the darkness came singing and rejoicing. Hundreds of thousands of escapees praised God for their deliverance and celebrated his goodness. Helicopters carried older people and some who were disabled, but most lined up for the walk that would lead them through the narrow passage to safety.

Sam looked for Mr. Stein, but he knew it would be too difficult to find one person in such a gathering. He guessed that Dr. Rosenzweig was somewhere preparing to speak to the throng. Sam could hardly contain his excitement over the prospect of welcoming Dr. Tsion Ben-Judah.

Nicolae Carpathia and his followers had tried to stop this gathering from ever happening. The shouts and cries of joy mocked the evil ruler and showed how impotent the world system was against the plans of God.

※

As night fell in Wisconsin, Vicki watched her friends head to their bunks or mattresses placed on the floor.

Colin had spoken briefly with Vicki about moving some of them to a church that had begun on the western side of the state. Vicki said she was open to it and that it was certainly needed, seeing how crowded the house had become. "But how do we choose who goes and who stays?"

"Let's talk about it in the morning," Colin said.

Shelly and Darrion stayed with Vicki until

late, then went to their cots. Vicki watched the continuing coverage with a sense of awe and terror. The love and protection of God overwhelmed her, but she couldn't believe people still clung to the hope that Nicolae Carpathia was the answer to the world's problems.

In the midst of stories about the bloody seas and the GC's defeat in the air over Israel, Vicki saw an announcement for those who had not taken the mark of Carpathia. New application sites were opening, and Dr. Neal Damosa had scheduled a young people's rally at different sites around the world where kids could watch the next day's celebration *and* receive the mark.

Vicki shook her head. Only the Global Community could celebrate when there was so much death and destruction.

The motion alarm rang again and Vicki quickly flipped a switch, turning it off. She pulled up video of different sensors around Colin's property and noticed something moving in one of the frames. She enlarged the picture and saw an animal with a long tail crawling up a tree near the camera. She focused on the two eyes and long snout and recognized an opossum, with several little ones clinging to its back. The animal moved up and out of the frame and Vicki smiled. They were ugly creatures, but the babies were sort of cute.

The sensor beeped again so Vicki clicked back to the full list of camera shots. Some showed the dim glow of lights in houses several hundred yards away. The activated sensors were in the wooded area behind the house.

Vicki was about to turn everything off and go to bed when something caught her eye in a corner of the screen. A tree branch moved. Was it the wind? She enlarged the picture and moved closer. The image was grainy and slightly green.

A shadow moved in the moonlight. Was it another animal?

Vicki noticed something strange hanging behind one of the branches. At first it looked like Spanish moss, but the more she studied it, the more convinced she became that it was moving forward. The branch moved again—was that someone's arm?

A face!

It filled the screen, and long, black hair covered the camera. Vicki jumped back and knocked some books off the table behind her. When she turned, the screen was blank.

※

Judd awoke early to a flurry of activity in the hotel room. Though it was still dark, Westin had a bag packed and Lionel was eating a bagel and some fruit he had brought from downstairs.

"Get dressed," Westin said. "It's time to go."

Westin took them underground to the Humvee and they drove into the smoky streets. Debris from downed choppers littered the roadside. Rescue crews worked on several buildings damaged by falling aircraft.

"Did you talk with Z-Van?" Lionel said.

Westin shook his head. "I didn't want him to know I was in town. But I did see his buddy, Lars Rahlmost."

"The guy making that movie about Nicolae's resurrection?" Judd said.

"Yeah. And he says he got some great footage last night. He's supposed to be at the celebration this morning, but I have my doubts about them pulling it off, what with half the GC troops injured or unaccounted for."

Judd's heart raced as they neared the airport. When they were back with their friends, they wouldn't have to worry about Carpathia's attacks. Judd was sure there would be danger, but nothing like they had seen in

Israel and New Babylon. He didn't know how Chang could stand working in the same building with the most evil man on earth.

Judd thought of Vicki. He hoped she hadn't changed her mind about him. She had seemed excited about the possibility of them working on their relationship, and he wanted one more chance to prove himself.

Westin pointed out more wreckage, and Judd feared there might be debris on the airport runway. He sighed when a plane rose into the air.

"Won't be long now," Westin said.

They returned the Humvee and took a shuttle to the terminal. Westin showed his pass at the checkpoint and located the hangar where Z-Van's plane was stored. The three jogged toward it.

"I'm going to get in touch with Chang as soon as we're in the air," Judd said.

Westin stopped. "Oh no."

"What's wrong?" Judd said.

Westin gestured to the hangar. From the side it had looked okay, but now, as they neared the front, Judd saw a gaping hole in the roof and emergency crews at work.

The familiar insignia of The Four Horsemen lay on the ground, burning.

Z-Van's plane had been destroyed.

ABOUT THE AUTHORS

Jerry B. Jenkins (www.jerryjenkins.com) is the writer of the Left Behind series. He owns the Jerry B. Jenkins Christian Writers Guild, an organization dedicated to mentoring aspiring authors. Former vice president for publishing for the Moody Bible Institute of Chicago, he also served many years as editor of *Moody* magazine and is now Moody's writer-at-large.

His writing has appeared in publications as varied as *Reader's Digest, Parade, Guideposts,* in-flight magazines, and dozens of other periodicals. Jenkins's biographies include books with Billy Graham, Hank Aaron, Bill Gaither, Luis Palau, Walter Payton, Orel Hershiser, and Nolan Ryan, among many others. His books appear regularly on the *New York Times, USA Today, Wall Street Journal,* and *Publishers Weekly* best-seller lists.

Jerry is also the writer of the nationally syndicated sports story comic strip *Gil Thorp,* distributed to newspapers across the United States by Tribune Media Services.

Jerry and his wife, Dianna, live in Colorado and have three grown sons.

Dr. Tim LaHaye (www.timlahaye.com), who conceived the idea of fictionalizing an account of the Rapture and the Tribulation, is a noted author, minister, and nationally recognized speaker on Bible prophecy. He is the founder of both Tim LaHaye Ministries and The PreTrib Research Center. He also recently cofounded the Tim LaHaye School of Prophecy at Liberty University. Presently Dr. LaHaye speaks at many of the major Bible prophecy conferences in the U.S. and Canada, where his current prophecy books are very popular.

Dr. LaHaye holds a doctor of ministry degree from Western Theological Seminary and a doctor of literature degree from Liberty University. For twenty-five years he pastored one of the nation's outstanding churches in San Diego, which grew to three locations. It was during that time that he founded two accredited Christian high schools, a Christian school system of ten schools, and Christian Heritage College.

Dr. LaHaye has written over forty books that have been published in more than thirty languages. He has written books on a wide variety of subjects, such as family life, temperaments, and Bible prophecy. His current fiction works, the Left Behind series, written with Jerry B. Jenkins, continue to appear on the bestseller lists of the Christian Booksellers Association, *Publishers Weekly*, *Wall Street Journal*, *USA Today*, and the *New York Times*.

He is the father of four grown children and grandfather of nine. Snow skiing, waterskiing, motorcycling, golfing, vacationing with family, and jogging are among his leisure activities.

The Future Is Clear

Check out the exciting Left Behind: The Kids series

BOOKS #33 AND #34 COMING SOON!

Hooked on the exciting
Left Behind: The Kids series?
Then you'll love the dramatic audios!

Listen as the characters come to life in this theatrical
audio that makes the saga of those left behind
even more exciting.

High-tech sound effects, original music,
and professional actors will have you
on the edge of your seat.

Experience the heart-stopping action and
suspense of the end times for yourself!

Three exciting volumes available on CD or cassette.